Luigi, who lives on the Street of the Strangers in the French city of Marseilles, believes that a gypsy has put a curse on his family. He is convinced when his sister, Doro, has an accident and, although the doctors pronounce her well, she insists she cannot walk. The efforts of Luigi, Mamma, and their friends—Madame and Signor Gamba and their monkey, Fifino; Laila Najjar, the Arab dancing girl; the Senegalese couple; Mouky, the gypsy boy; and many others—to encourage her back to health are both humorous and touching.

Against a vivid background of assorted tongues, smells, and sounds, Mrs. Carlson has created an exciting and colorful story, punctuated with the gentle humor and affection of the Valli family. Emily Arnold McCully's illustrations skillfully catch the ceaseless movement of the old Mediterranean port and all its heterogeneous inhabitants.

United States nominee for the 1966 renowned Hans Christian Andersen Award.

ABOUT THE ARTIST

The talented young artist, Emily Arnold McCully, a newcomer to the field of children's books, is also recognized for her work in magazine illustration and jackets for paperback and hard-cover books. Born in Galesburg, Illinois, she received a bachelor's degree from Brown University, was elected to Phi Beta Kappa there, and later earned a master's degree in art history from Columbia University. She now lives in Pennsylvania with her husband, George, a professor of Renaissance and Reformation history at Swarthmore College.

*Other Books by Natalie Savage Carlson*

A Brother for the Orphelines
Carnival in Paris
Chalou
The Empty Schoolhouse
The Family Under the Bridge
The Happy Orpheline
Jean-Claude's Island
The Letter on the Tree
The Orphelines in the Enchanted Castle
A Pet for the Orphelines
Sailor's Choice
Sashes Red and Blue
The Song of the Lop-Eared Mule
The Talking Cat
The Tomahawk Family
Wings Against the Wind

# » LUIGI
## OF THE STREETS

VINS
BIERES
RUE
des
ETRANGERS

*Pictures by Emily Arnold McCully*

# » LUIGI OF THE STREETS

by Natalie Savage Carlson

Harper & Row, Publishers · New York, Evanston, and London

LUIGI OF THE STREETS

LIBRARY OF CONGRESS CATALOG CARD NUMBER: 67-16479

In memory of Josine Kay Leutscher,
a wonderful little girl I would like to have known

# » Contents

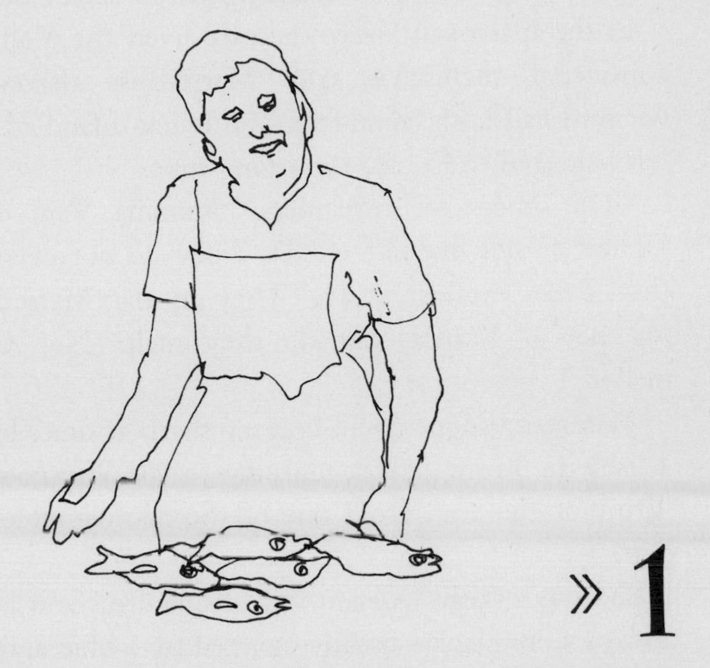

# »1

# The Street of the Strangers

In the French city of Marseilles on the Mediterranean Sea was a narrow cobbled way called the Street of the Strangers. It was shut in by gray walls and shopfronts that were the color of faded flowers.

The name was fitting because most of the tenants were Arabs

from Algeria. Halfway down the street was the Café Oasis. Its blue archway was covered with scalloped Arabic writing. Pictures of Laila Najjar, the dancing girl, were in the window.

In the apartment above the café lived the Valli family. They considered themselves true Marseillais, although Papà and Mamma had both come from the Italian island of Corsica which has belonged to France for a long time.

"The others are foreigners," Mamma Valli often declared. "They do not live like we do. They do not even think like we do—if they think at all. Ha! They say that Marseilles is the melting pot of France, but do they melt? No! Only we have melted."

Mamma's tongue could be very sharp at times because she was a fishwife. From earliest morning to late afternoon she sold her "fruit of the sea" from one of the market tables near the old port.

She was a large woman with strong arms and heavy feet. She always wore black—usually covered by a blue apron. No matter how hard she scrubbed them, her clothes always smelled of fish.

"We must smell like mermaids." She often joked with the Italian woman who presided over the next table in the market.

Mamma tramped across the floor and glanced through the window which was closed against the November cold.

The view was one of sagging shutters and crooked lines of wash festooning the windows. The street below was often filled with Algerian men in French clothing. Sometimes there was a woman, half drawing a scarf across her face as if she were still in Africa. Occasionally the statuesque Senegalese woman with skin like polished ebony strode past with a basket on her head and a baby on her hip.

"See!" Mamma Valli pointed. "There is that old man in his heathen sheets, sitting on the sidewalk with his chickens. Have his ways melted since he left Africa?"

Luigi, her eleven-year-old son, ran to her side. He was a slim boy with large ears and a blackbird wing of hair across his forehead. He could have passed for one of the Arab boys.

He looked through the window too, at the old Algerian sitting in front of his poultry shop. He was wrapped tightly in his burnoose, and his pocked nose and white beard poked out of its hood. He sat with his gnarled fingers clutching the legs of two scrawny chickens, imploring the passers to buy them.

Doro, two years younger than Luigi, stayed at the table finishing a slice of cheese.

"Oush!" she exclaimed with a shudder. "I hate him. Every time I pass by, he grabs at my ankles as if I am a chicken he is trying to catch. He squawks at me, 'Who are you? What is your name?' Then I run past him as fast as I can."

"I like Yussuf." Luigi defended the old chicken seller. "It is a game he plays with me. I am supposed to answer, 'I am Luigi.' Then he asks, 'The son of whom?' and I say, 'Luigi, the son of

Dorotea.' 'The daughter of whom?' 'The daughter of Julio. I am Luigi, the son of Dorotea, the daughter of Julio.' That's the way the Arabs do it."

"You will please leave me and your grandfather out of anything Arab," ordered Mamma. "And when I passed the corner coming home I saw that gypsy boy in his rags. It is a shame the way his people leave him there all day to beg in such cold weather."

Doro raised her curly head with more interest. She was small for her age with great Madonna eyes and earrings that glistened like golden teardrops.

"I feel sorry for Mouky," she said. "They wouldn't let the gypsies camp in a village during a terrible windstorm. If they had let Mouky's family stay there, the van wouldn't have blown over and crippled his legs. That's what he says."

"If his family had stayed in one place like decent people," said Mamma, "such a thing never would have happened."

Mouky was a familiar sight on the street corner. His family had sought shelter in town for the winter, renting an empty loft while the older men went to work in the soap factory. Every day the boy sat at the corner in a box on skate wheels that was so low he could push himself about with his hands. He called it his *pousse-pousse*. In a high, whining voice he begged for coins to be dropped into his tin cup.

"Mouky is my friend," said Luigi. "It makes me mad to see the way his parents quarrel with him every morning when they carry him there. I don't think he likes to beg."

"Once I gave him a sou I found in the gutter," said Doro, "and he was so polite. He wished me a long life and riches."

"Ho! Riches will not come to a foolish child who squanders money on beggars." Mamma was forgetting that she herself often gave the boy a small coin on days when she had good sales. "If you had to work for your money, my little one, as I have worked since Papà's death, you would realize that."

A sadness fell over the three as all eyes were turned toward the picture hanging over the clock shelf. It was a young Papà with a handsome moustache that curled elegantly at the ends, and gay, sparkling eyes. There was a lock of his curly black hair pressed between the picture and the glass. Doro had inherited his curls and Luigi his bright eyes.

Papà had been a dock worker—one of the strongest. If that ship's winch hadn't broken and the great sacks of copra fallen on him . . .

"But it is time for you to return to school," said Mamma briskly. "And after I have cleared this mess of dishes, I must go back to the market. You are lucky children to have a mamma who comes home to get you a hot lunch. Most of the other women bring a snack to eat at their tables or go to the café on the corner. I would have to do the same if it wasn't for good Madame Gamba who keeps an eye on my fish. Before I leave, I fetch her a bowl of warm soup from the café. We help each other. You should play with her boy more, Luigi, instead of roving the streets with Arab vagabonds who get you into trouble with the police."

"I play with Guido sometimes," said Luigi, reaching for his torn jacket, "but he won't have anything to do with the Arabs. He calls them *figuiers* and that makes them fight. I'd fight too if somebody called me a fig tree."

"I see no insult in that," said his mother. "A fig tree is noble. It bears rich fruit."

"But he means it as an insult," explained Luigi. "He means that they come from Africa where there are many fig trees and that lazy Arabs sit under them all day. And the Arabs know he means that. What would you do if someone called *you* a fig tree?"

"Ha! I should let him have a fish across his face," boasted Mamma, "although I still see nothing wrong in it."

Luigi ducked out the door, raced down the steep stairs and through the cramped hallway until he reached the street.

He usually waited for Doro, but today he was running away from her. He wasn't going to walk back to school with her this afternoon—to the forbidding high-walled building with one entrance for boys and the other for girls. He did not intend to go back to school at all. He wasn't even going to cut school with the Arab boys. Something exciting had come up.

Of course he would have to walk several blocks in order to

avoid meeting his mother or Doro. Then he would retrace his steps to the corner where Mouky was staked out to beg.

The gypsy boy was going to let him ride his *pousse-pousse* down a nearby street that was steep and winding.

It would be great sport. Luigi loved to ride things that went fast. That is why he often stole rides on the rear ends of automobiles and trucks. It was daring and risky, but he courted danger and excitement. He had been urging Doro to join him in this pastime although she was a timid little thing.

But today he was not going to share Mouky's *pousse-pousse* with anyone—not with Doro or the Arabs.

Luigi loved the city streets. To him the tall, shuttered buildings were castles to be explored. He did this by sneaking up the steps of strange rooming houses and prowling the dark halls until evicted by the portress or one of the tenants. There was buried treasure to be found in trash bins and dumps. And the policemen in their trim uniforms were enemies to be outwitted.

In the Valli apartment Luigi was only a boy bossed by his mother and watched by his sister. But in the endless maze of mysterious alleyways he could be a brave soldier of the Foreign Legion stalking Moorish bandits or a Moorish bandit eluding the Legionnaires.

As he raced past, the old Arab, Yussuf, snatched at his feet. "Who are you?" he demanded. "What is your name?"

But Luigi did not answer, "I am Luigi, son of Dorotea, daughter of Julio." He was in too much of a hurry. And he wasn't Luigi. He was the favorite driver about to enter the great race of the Rallye de Monte Carlo. There would be breakneck speed and death-defying curves and near crack-ups. There would be magnificent danger—especially if the after-lunch traffic had thickened on the main street below.

It so happened that Mouky didn't know yet that he was going to lend his *pousse-pousse* to Luigi. But Luigi had his strategy well-planned.

He squeezed through a broken wall and went to a pile of rubble left by the wreckers tearing down an old building. It made a safe cache for treasures.

Luigi dug into a landslide of broken concrete and dragged out a strange piece of rusted hardware. It was shaped like a centipede with many thin iron branches. Bolts were screwed on the ends of three.

He had found it on the dock when he and the Arab boys had been playing pirates among the mounds of wheat sacks and monuments of orange crates that had just been unloaded from Oran.

The value of it was enhanced because nobody could guess what it was for—not even Ali, son of Ahmed, whose father made queer little twists of wire and clever metal hooks for coaxing locks and prying windows.

It might turn out to be something very important. Perhaps it was so important that a great search was on to find it. Perhaps even the police were looking for it—whatever it was. That would make it even more valuable—like smuggled jewels or tobacco.

Luigi sought out his gypsy friend.

"Look what I found!" he exclaimed, triumphantly producing the iron puzzle.

The gypsy boy was immediately interested. "What is it?" he asked, his dark fingers reverently caressing the rusty object.

"I don't know," replied Luigi proudly. "Nobody knows. It could be almost anything. I found it down on the dock, so perhaps it came all the way from Haifa or Dakar, perhaps even from America."

Mouky's eyes shone. His father sometimes forged horseshoes and nails. But Mouky was sure that his father had never seen anything just like this.

"It might be a charm," suggested the gypsy. "Perhaps one can cast spells with it."

"Could be," admitted Luigi. "I bet the owner is looking all over for it. See here! This bolt really screws off." He demonstrated that the bolt worked.

"This one is stuck," said Mouky.

"Because it's so rusted," explained Luigi. "If you spit on it a couple times, it might loosen. I bet this thing has been lost a donkey's lifetime—whatever it is. I bet somebody has been looking for it a long time."

Mouky was overcome by greed. "I'll give you one of my coins for it." He rattled his cup temptingly.

"No," said Luigi. "It wouldn't be right to take your money. And if your parents found out, they might beat you."

"They won't find out," promised Mouky. "They don't know how much money I have until they pick me up."

"It wouldn't be honest," said Luigi piously.

The gypsy boy was not daunted. "I could get one of my mother's bracelets for you," he suggested. "I know where she puts them at night."

"What would I do with a bracelet?" asked Luigi in disgust.

"You could give it to your sister. She is a girl of kind heart, and I would like for her to have it."

"My sister wouldn't wear a stolen bracelet."

Mouky looked hurt. "I wouldn't steal it," he said. "I would only borrow it. And if I forget to return it . . ." He shrugged this thin shoulders.

Luigi played with the iron piece for a few moments. "I tell you what," he said as if he had a sudden inspiration. "I know something that won't cost you a sou. I'll give you this thing if you'll let me borrow your *pousse-pousse* and coast down the hill."

As Luigi had expected, such a businesslike arrangement was irresistible to Mouky.

"But it won't be like borrowing my mother's bracelet, will it?"

he asked cautiously. "You won't forget to return it? Papa may come early for me today. He isn't working at the factory."

Luigi agreed. He helped Mouky out of the low wagon and set him against a lamp post.

He dragged the *pousse-pousse* along until he came to the steep, winding street. Then he gave the box a great shove and jumped in. He braced his feet against the front board with his knees drawn up under his chin. The great Rallye de Monte Carlo was off!

The skate wheels turned and the box gained momentum. He was fairly flying down the steep hill. The wheels clattered over the cobblestones, making Luigi's feet and bottom feel numb and his teeth chatter. It was a delicious feeling.

Pedestrians who had taken to the middle of the street jumped to the sidewalk and into doorways. He had a fleeting glimpse of fists shaking at him. On, on clattered the *pousse-pousse*, past bicycles and slow-moving automobiles. The daring racer was passing all of his rivals.

Luigi tried to use his hands to guide the *pousse-pousse* as he had seen Mouky do. But the little cart had become a runaway.

He shut his eyes at the next intersection. If he had kept them open, he would have seen a truck swerve up onto the sidewalks to avoid hitting him. A young girl crossing the street in her high heels changed her mind and jumped back on the bare toes of a brown-robed monk. A shopper coming home from the market dropped her purchases into the gutter, and a man pushing a barrow of eggplants pushed them right into the middle of a flower stand.

Ah! Luigi would surely win the coveted trophy and all of France would cheer.

But alas! He did not know that the street ended in broad stone steps. The *pousse-pousse* jolted down four of them, knocked against the iron railing, and sent the dauntless racer sprawling on the fifth step.

A brawny fisherman in rubber boots hurried to the boy and helped him up.

"Are you badly hurt, poor boy?" he kept asking over and over while Luigi rubbed his knee with one hand and the side of his face with the other.

"No, monsieur." Luigi decided that he was bruised but unbroken. "But I have lost the race."

When the fisherman learned that the boy had no broken bones, his entire manner changed. The hand that so tenderly remained on Luigi's shoulder now began shaking him as violently as if he were still riding over the cobbles.

"Wicked boy!" screeched the man. "You deserve a beating for such mischief. You should be put in jail."

An old woman who did not know what had happened came up and began belaboring the man with her cane. "Villain!" she

COUILLON FR
BIÈRES
Pousse-Pousse

cried. "Shame on you for punishing your son so roughly. You should reason with him."

More people began gathering. Luigi was panic-stricken. A crowd always attracted a policeman. He jumped away once his supposed father had let go of him to ward off the blows from the cane. He had the presence of mind to grab hold of the *pousse-pousse*. Then he ran down another block with it banging behind him, and plodded back up the hill by a half-hidden alley.

When he felt that his trail had been covered, he turned his attention to the cart. One corner was splintered and a wheel gone. He didn't dare go back to look for the wheel.

With dawdling feet he returned to the gypsy boy's corner. Oh, weren't things ever so bad that they couldn't get worse? Mouky's father was with him. He was giving his son the same kind of shaking that Luigi had received from the strong fisherman.

Luigi's first impulse was to let go of the *pousse-pousse* and run. But such cowardice did not seem worthy of a game loser at the moment. Especially since it was not likely the gypsies would want police intervention. So he slowly approached Mouky and his father, lugging the cart by one wheel.

"Is this what you're looking for?" he boldly asked the swarthy gypsy father. "I only borrowed it for a few minutes."

At sight of the broken cart the man acted as if he were being tortured in a dungeon. He screamed and tore at his greasy black hair. He burst into a torrent of Gitan language. Then with blazing eyes he raised his fist over the boy. Luigi ducked the blow which he expected. But the gypsy man only opened his fingers and made signs in the air as if he were tracing invisible words.

Cold terror chilled Luigi. He was sure that Mouky's father was putting a curse on him. He ran home as fast as his feet would take him. The glory of the Rallye de Monte Carlo was over.

Then the mistral came down the Rhone valley like the wrath of a thousand gypsies. For three days the savage wind funneled through the streets, and even the old Arab stayed inside his poultry shop. The wind blew off a shutter in the Street of the Strangers and sent it splintering into the plate glass of the Café Oasis. It tore the pink dancing dress of Laila Najjar from the clothesline and sent it twirling and twisting down the street as if she were still in it.

When the wind's fury was spent, Luigi felt as if it had blown his problems away. Of course there had been an uproar over his having ditched school that afternoon. No one seemed to mind if the Arabs didn't come to school regularly, but let him miss half a day and you'd think that France was about to fall.

He had caught it from both Mamma and his teachers. But Mamma's scolding had been the worst because she had ended it by pointing to the picture on the wall.

"Papà is watching you," she said. "How ashamed he must be of his only son."

Luigi was glad that Papà's picture had not seen the shameful ending of his ride down the cobbles on Mouky's *pousse-pousse.*

After a few days he dared seek Mouky to explain about the little cart. He noticed that there was a new wheel on it, a fourth wheel which was not the same size as the others and made the cart list.

"Your father should have made it stronger," he said. "What would happen if *you* rolled away in it?"

Mouky was sullen. "A fine fellow you are," he declared. "You go off with my *pousse-pousse* and break it up. Then you leave me to face my father alone."

"Didn't you show him the piece of iron I gave you?"

Mouky spat over his shoulder. "He says it's junk."

"What was it he said to me when he was so mad?" asked Luigi fearfully. "Did he put a curse on me?"

Mouky confirmed his fears. "Yes. You will never grow any taller and your eyes will get crossed." Luigi felt relieved. He had feared something much worse than that. "And bad luck will come to your family," the other finished. "Papa is very good at curses. They always stick."

# » 2 The Waterfront

Luigi was uneasy about the gypsy curse that had been put on him. He took a pencil and made a mark on the door to the tiny bedroom shared by Mamma and Doro so that he could measure his growth from day to day. That part of the curse seemed to be working. In a week's time he had not grown any taller than the mark. Perhaps he would be a dwarf like Mustafa's uncle who played a flute in the orchestra at the Café Oasis.

Each day he would secretly go the mirror over the wobbly table to study his eyes. One looked higher than the other, but that was the fault of the mirror and nothing new. He made the interesting discovery that by looking down at his nose, he could cross his eyes himself. This ended his fear of that part of the curse. If they became crossed due to Mouky's father, he would just stop looking at his nose.

But there was that ominous thing about bad luck for his family. It was something one could not measure by a mark on the door or see in a mirror.

For almost a week Luigi was a model boy, mindful that Papà was watching him. He noticed a strange thing which made him sure of it. When he sat at the table eating his food, Papà's eyes were fastened on him. If he stood by the hall door, the same was true. Even as he walked across the floor, the keen eyes followed him.

"Why is Papà always looking at me?" the boy asked his sister one evening. "Why doesn't he ever look at you?"

Doro was surprised. "But he is looking straight at me right now."

"No, he isn't," Luigi corrected her. "He is looking at me."

Mamma stepped from the tiny kitchen corner that was separated from the main room by a striped drape like the one that hung in the doorway of the Café Oasis in the hot summertime.

"You are both wrong," she said. "Papà is looking at me."

Then she explained that this was because of the way the picture had been taken. Papà had looked straight into the camera. "You see he watches all of us," said Mamma, "so we must never do anything we wouldn't want him to see."

The next Sunday, Mass was letting out at the ancient stone church of St. Laurent near the harbor. A small crowd of fishermen and others who lived in the shadow of its bell tower walked across the parvis. The Vallis were among them, Mamma pulling the black shawl back from her head.

An old soldier with two medals on his chest had taken off his faded blue cap and was holding it out hopefully to one churchgoer after another.

"Alms for an old soldier who fought for France," he kept chanting. "Alms for an old soldier."

Mamma unsnapped her worn purse that also had a fishy smell.

"Here, Doro," she said. "Give the old soldier this sou. He fought for us."

As they started down the steps there was Mouky waiting with his tin cup.

"Charity for a poor crippled boy," he whined.

Mamma frowned. "If I give money to every beggar in Marseilles, I shall have to begin begging myself."

"Oh, please give poor Mouky some money," cried Doro. "It is so sad about him."

Her mother grudgingly opened the purse again. "I will not give as much in the collection next Sunday," she decided. "That will even up my charity."

"Blessings on you, little lady," said Mouky to Doro. "May you have a long life and riches."

"I wish I were rich enough to take you to a doctor who could fix your legs," said Doro.

"If his legs were cured, he wouldn't be able to beg anymore," reasoned Luigi. "Then how would he make money?"

"I would sell things like needles and thread from door to door," said Mouky. "I always wanted to do that."

Mamma noticed the tilt to the little cart.

"What happened to it?" she asked. "Did you have an accident?"

Mouky scowled. "A bad boy broke it."

Mamma was shocked. "Shame on him! It must have been a very bad boy who would break the cart of a cripple."

"Perhaps he didn't do it on purpose," said Luigi in a small voice.

Mouky ignored him. "He cheated me too," he added.

"How dreadful!" exclaimed Mamma. "A woman tried to cheat me at the market last week when she bought some of my mackerel. But I was on my guard because I saw from the first that she had an evil face."

Luigi made a note in his mind to look at himself in Mamma's mirror as soon as he reached home so he could see what an evil face looked like.

Mouky gave Luigi a slanted glance. "Bad luck will come to the boy's family."

"It surely will if his parents aren't stricter with him," declared Mamma indignantly. "These young Arabs are always getting into mischief."

Luigi's face colored. He wanted to change the subject.

"Let's take our walk," he suggested.

"Now that we're so close," added Mamma, "we might as well go down to the harbor and look at the ships."

Every Sunday, weather permitting, she took them for a promenade after Mass.

"We always did it when Papà was alive," she often said, "so we must keep up the custom."

As the Vallis walked away, Luigi turned back to Mouky and made his most evil face. He even looked down at his nose so it would be uglier.

The boy usually found the promenades dull and tried to get out of them so that he could play with his friends. But today he decided that he should go along to protect Mamma. Evidently the bad luck was not coming to Doro else the gypsy boy wouldn't have wished her riches and a long life. He must be watchful of Mamma to see that a load of copra didn't fall on *her*.

They reached the Quai de la Tourette and headed for the Joliette basin. Before them stretched the long flat-roofed warehouses, and giant cranes reached to the sky. Beyond was the blue, blue water of the Mediterranean Sea, man-made into a harbor by endless lines of seawalls and jetties. Even farther away was the green and white curve of the hills of southern Provence.

Since it was Sunday, there was not the usual bustle and din on the docks. But little coastal vessels were discharging crowds of deck passengers, and a great liner cast off its lines for the voyage to Egypt. The mingled smells of many cargoes spiced the air.

The Vallis were so busy staring at the ships that Mamma stumbled over a coil of rope and fell down. Luigi helped her up as best he could by tugging at her coat and shawl. He dusted off her coat. Doro picked up the handbag she had dropped and handed it back to her.

"You aren't hurt are you, Mamma?" Luigi asked anxiously. "You didn't break your leg, did you? Are you sure you are all right?"

"I am clumsy," said Mamma. "I must watch where I'm going."

Luigi took her chapped red hand protectively. "Don't bump into that crane," he warned.

They turned down a finger pier to look at more ships. Luigi was interested in their size and the flags they carried, but Doro took delight in reading the names.

"The *Foulaya* from Singapore," she cried. "It needs painting."

"See, it has brought bags of rice." Luigi pointed to the sacks piled on the pier.

"They ship their rice to us and we send them back rice from our Camargue," said Mamma. "It's a very fair exchange."

She stepped closer to look at the ship.

"Take care, Mamma," warned Luigi. "You might fall into the water."

Mamma pointed excitedly. "There is the *Napoleon* from my Corsica docking. She is surely bringing olive oil and chestnuts. All the cooks in Marseilles will rejoice over that cargo."

A group of French sailors at liberty came wandering aimlessly like a flock of sea gulls out of their element on land.

"Someday you will be a *matelot* like one of them," Mamma said proudly to Luigi. "Or perhaps you may be a brave soldier when you reach the age for your military service."

That seemed a very far off time to Luigi.

"Oh, please be a sailor," urged Doro. "I love the red pompons on their caps."

"I'll be a sailor if soldiers end up begging at churches," promised Luigi.

They came to the *Huguette* of Marseilles being loaded by a gang of Algerians working overtime. The men were fastening slings around the shiny body of a brand new automobile that had been manufactured in Paris. After much shouting and confusion, the snarling winch strained the cable. The slings tightened and the automobile slowly rose in the air.

"I wish I were in that auto," said Luigi. "It would be like riding in an airplane." He eagerly asked one of the workers, "May I ride up in the next one?"

The man gave Luigi a lopsided grin. "You want to go to Casablanca?" he asked. He pointed to a waiting car. "You get in and drive it across the Mediterranean. If you get there, you keep the car."

The other men laughed as if it were a great joke. This encouraged the joker.

"Perhaps your mother wants a ride up," he suggested.

"She'd break the cable," snickered one.

"The ship would sink," said another.

Mamma let go of Luigi's hand and clenched her fists. The boy was alarmed. If Mamma hit the men, that surely would bring bad luck to her.

"Come, Mamma," he urged. "Let's go and see that freighter over there."

Mamma huffily straightened her back and walked away with

great dignity. But before she went far, she turned to shout, "Fig trees!"

"Don't pay any attention to them," cried Luigi. "Hurry up!"

He was filled with fright. Now all the Arabs would be mad at Mamma. He looked back to make sure that none of them was drawing a knife on her. But they were only laughing among themselves.

"Big camel!" one of them called.

Mamma held her head high. "These Arabs are very rude," she remarked. "And on Sunday."

"Friday is their Sunday," Luigi informed her in defense of the Muslim Algerians. He strove to draw her attention away from them. "Look! The *Leptis* from Dakar has brought peanuts because they grow in Senegal. That's what is in those big yellow sacks. I wonder where—o-oh, look! Monkeys!"

There were cages of them near the wall of the terminal. It seemed most fitting that the *Leptis* had combined monkeys with peanuts.

A man had just finished watering the animals when the Valli children rushed over.

"Where are they going?" asked Luigi excitedly. "I wish I had one. Are they tame?"

The man fastened the door to the last cage securely and picked up his empty pail. "They're going to zoos all over Europe," he told him. "But look good at that sign."

The sign said: SAVAGE BEASTS. DO NOT MOLEST.

This didn't bother Luigi. As soon as the man was gone, he jabbed his forefinger between the bars and tickled a little brown monkey.

"He looks like Fifino, doesn't he?" he asked his sister.

Fifino was the monkey that belonged to Guido Gamba's grandfather. The old man wandered the streets with a hand organ, accompanied by Fifino in a clever little Zouave uniform with baggy purple pants and a cunning red cap. It was mainly because of Fifino that Luigi played with Guido at all. Old Signor Gamba sometimes allowed the boys to take the monkey for a walk.

"Do you think that Fifino came from Dakar in a big ship?" asked Doro.

The monkey jabbered and wrung his tiny hands as if he were trying to answer her question. Then he took Luigi's finger in his paw and studied it intently before he let go.

"He really seems tame," said Mamma. She, too, put her finger through the bars. "How goes it, Fifino?"

The monkey took hold of her finger and stared at the broken nail. He scratched his head and the Vallis roared with laughter. Then he suddenly pulled Mamma's finger to his mouth and bit it.

She gave a scream and jerked away. She looked at the drops of blood and the tiny red tooth marks on the end of her finger. She sucked on it. The monkey screeched gleefully.

"The little savage!" Mamma declared. "I should bite him back. That would teach him a lesson in politeness."

Luigi seized her other hand. "No, no, Mamma! Please let's go." He began pulling on her arm with all his might. "Come on home, Mamma," he implored. "I don't want to walk anymore."

He must get her away from the dangerous harbor before something worse happened to her.

They went home by way of the Quai du Port. The old harbor bristled with the masts of little fishing boats. Among them gay white yachts danced on the ripples.

During the war the Germans had destroyed the slums along the north side of the harbor. Now it was lined by new apartment houses. They were like giant concrete blocks. The windows were square. The doorways were square. The balconies were square.

"They say there are fine apartments for workers in them," said Mamma, "with plenty of room and modern conveniences. But I don't think I should like to live in one. I would feel quite square myself—and I would rather be round like a camel."

Mamma's good humor had returned, but Luigi did not feel safe until they reached the Street of the Strangers. It was a good thing that he had stayed with her for the promenade. If it hadn't been for him, worse luck than a monkey bite surely would have overtaken her.

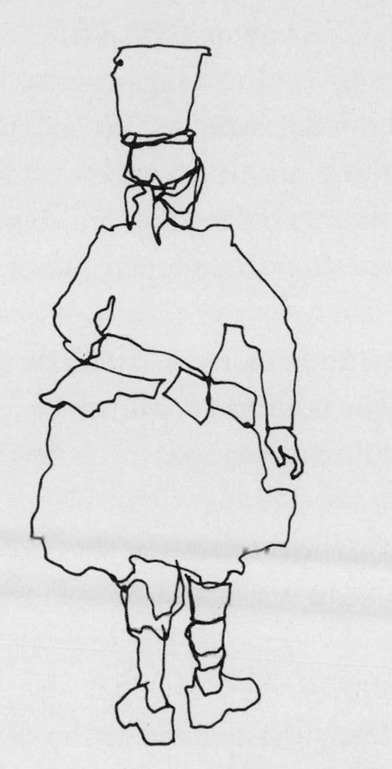

# » 3

## The Stolen Ride

Mamma almost ran into bad luck the very next day. She was coming home from the Quai de Rive Neuve with a basket of the sardines which the fishermen had found plentiful in the waters off La Ciotat. The nets had been so heavy with them that a fisherman had given her two dozen when his boat tied up in the old port.

On top of them Mamma had placed the big mackerel left over from her own sales. There would be a fish feast tonight with sardines fried in olive oil and the big mackerel spiced with garlic.

As she turned into the Street of the Strangers, she saw Laila Najjar coming toward her. The curly-headed girl strode along gracefully in her short woolen skirt and baggy sweater. An aura of heavy oriental perfume enveloped her. Her bare face, which had never known the veil, was pretty despite the two big tattoo marks on her forehead. Doro particularly admired the marks. Once she had tried to copy them on her own face with a crayon, but her teacher had made her go to the washroom and clean her forehead.

As the girl approached Mamma, she looked at the basket of fish in her arms. Then she instinctively put her fingers to her nose.

Mamma was insulted. She grabbed the shiny mackerel and threw it at Laila. The girl screamed as the slimy fish hit her, then she ran away as fast as she could.

A young Arab man who had witnessed the scene darted out of a doorway, seized the fish from the cobbles, and disappeared into the rooming house.

Old Yussuf on the sidewalk among the chicken coops cackled with laughter.

They were not the only ones who had seen Mamma's encounter. Luigi had been watching for her from the window. He was fearful that she might have been run over by a truck or fallen into the water.

He raced down the steps and out the door.

"Mamma, you shouldn't have done that," he admonished her as he took the basket. "Now you will have enemies right on our street."

"No, I shouldn't have done it," said Mamma contritely. "I have wasted my mackerel and it was such a lovely fish."

Luigi even sought Yussuf's help. "Will you please keep an eye on my mother, Dorotea, when she is in the street?" he asked the chicken-seller. "She sometimes gets excited and does things she doesn't really mean."

The Arab's wrinkles knotted into a deep grin. "It seems to me, Luigi, son of Dorotea," he said, "that your mother is well able to take care of herself. But I will do as you ask. Allah preserve her."

But no one bothered them after the incident. Gradually Luigi relaxed his close surveillance of his mother. His restless mind couldn't stay on one thing long.

He even forgot that Papà was watching him when the next Saturday came around. He and Doro always had breakfast alone because their mother had to go to the quay long before daybreak to get her fish. Breakfast was easy because she always had the coffee made, and Doro ran down to the bakery for bread, with her coat over her long nightgown.

"Why bother going to school for only half a day?" Luigi tempted his sister. "Let's go on the Canebière. There's always something doing there."

Doro was uncertain for a few moments. "But we'll get into trouble at school."

"That won't be until next Monday," said Luigi. "We'll think of some excuse before then."

The temptation was too much for Doro. "And there will be the flower market there this morning. I love to look at the pretty flowers and smell them. I wish Mamma sold flowers instead of fish."

"Zut! You can't eat leftover flowers."

The Canebière is the most famous street in Marseilles. Its *allées* are flanked by ancient plane trees. Luxurious stores, hotels, and restaurants border its wide sidewalks. The Marseillais say that if Paris had a Canebière, it would be a little Marseilles.

This day the plane trees were bare, and the café tables and chairs had been moved inside. But bustling crowds and noisy vehicles enlivened the avenue.

The children walked slowly, savoring each new sight with relish. They enviously peeked into the café windows. At one, they watched a woman eating a roll and breaking off bits for the white Pekingese that occupied the chair next to her.

"I hope Mamma brings home some *croissants* just like those for lunch," said Doro, "and I hope they'll be fresh this time."

"I'd rather have a cup of that coffee to warm me up," said Luigi.

They watched each mouthful disappear until a haughty waiter came to the window and flicked his marshmallow-white napkin at them as if he were shooing away a pair of alley kittens.

Luigi impishly flattened his nose against the glass and crossed his eyes at the waiter before he left.

They went on until Doro was attracted by the display in a big store window. Christmas ornaments hung from a lighted chandelier. Under it were mannequins in exquisite gowns of silk and satin with furs draped over their shoulders. Their noses were tilted in scorn, as if they too despised the poorly dressed children. Doro could imagine the proud lady in the golden dress, saying, "Who let these dreadful children come to our Christmas party?"

"Come on," urged Luigi. "I don't want to waste my time looking at silly clothes."

But Doro was enthralled. It was as if something wonderful were about to happen at the party and the mannequins were breathlessly waiting. Perhaps the drapes in back would open and Pére Noël would enter with a bag full of jewels. Or perhaps Laila Najjar would dance through them in the pink costume she wore at the Café Oasis.

Even as Doro breathlessly waited too, the drapes rippled. From them stepped a clerk in a plain black suit with pins in his mouth. He went to the mannequin in the gold dress and took the fur stole from her shoulders. He began to unfasten one of her arms.

The spell was broken. "I'm ready to go now," said Doro. "They're only made of plaster."

When they reached the flower market, it was as if spring had come to Marseilles. Everywhere were bouquets of carnations and roses, buckets of mimosa and eucalyptus, and pots of hyacinths and tulips. There were even blooms that had come from such far islands that many people did not know their names.

"It smells like heaven," said Doro. She leaned over, closed her eyes, and buried her nose in a cluster of pink roses. "I wish our apartment smelled like this."

"I'd rather smell bouillabaisse cooking on the stove," Luigi disagreed with her. "Thick with fish and full of garlic."

The flower vendor, a girl in ski pants with her yellow hair puffed like a cheese soufflé, frowned at Doro. "Don't sniffle over the flowers, little girl," she scolded.

"Come on." Luigi pulled at his sister's sweater. "Who wants to smell flowers? Let's go back to the Rue de Rome and find some excitement. Let's catch a ride on the back of an auto. I'll teach you how today."

A nervous chill ran through Doro as she turned away from the roses. "Today?" she asked hesitantly. "Let's wait until another time."

"That's what you always say. It's today or never."

When they stood on the corner of the Canebière and the Rue de Rome and looked at the milling traffic, Doro tried to keep her teeth from chattering. "Maybe we *should* wait until some other time," she demurred. "Maybe we ought to go on home now that we're this near."

Luigi was impatient. "What's the matter? Are you one of old Yussuf's chickens?"

Doro felt that she was, but she didn't want Luigi to suspect it. "All right," she reluctantly agreed, "but how will I know what to do?"

"There's nothing to it, but there are too many *flics* here." Luigi's sharp eyes noticed two policemen. "We'll walk down to the next auto stop. When the traffic slows down, I'll pick out a car for you. One of those little closed vans will be best. The driver can't see you, and there is a step for your feet and the handle of the door to hang on to." He swaggered as he walked. "I've done it so much I just run out and jump on the trunk of a car that's got nothing to hold to. It's more exciting that way."

Doro's eyes widened with admiration for such daring. "How do I get off then?" she asked.

"The way you got on. Ride as long as you want, then when the car slows down at a corner or stops for a light, jump off. Then catch a ride back the same way."

He led her by the hand, and they stepped down into the gutter at the next auto stop. Doro's heart seemed to be beating in her ears.

"There's a good one," cried Luigi. He pushed Doro toward a delivery truck. But the girl pulled back.

"It—it's going too fast," she quavered.

They waited for another opportunity. "There!" shouted Luigi. "That one coming. It's going to stop."

But still Doro held back.

"You *are* a chicken," declared Luigi scornfully. "You'll just have to get a cold start."

He pulled her back on the sidewalk and led her down the street. He kept eyeing the parked cars. "We'll wait until somebody gets into one and starts the motor. There! That one! A man is getting into that florist van. It's just the one for you since you like to smell flowers."

This was easier for Doro. She hopped on the narrow back step and gripped the metal handle of the door with her right hand. Through the little window she could see masses of the market flowers.

The step jiggled and the van began to move. Doro was filled with sudden terror. She wanted to jump off, but she didn't dare as long as Luigi was watching her from the sidewalk. As the van slipped into the lane of traffic, she hung on for dear life. Now she was in the middle of a stampede of honking, roaring cars. A giant autobus almost grazed the van as it swung in toward the auto-stop sign. They picked up speed and the van wove through traffic lanes in a dizzying pattern. The step under Doro's feet jounced and the handle rattled in her fist.

She tried not to look at the traffic engulfing her. She fastened her eyes on the flowers inside the window. They were swaying back and forth as if growing in a windswept garden. She didn't even see Castellane Square with its fountain, or the handsome buildings and triple rows of plane trees along the broad Avenue du Prado.

Then the fingers gripping the handle grew tired and cramped, but Doro did not dare let go long enough to change hands. Luigi had told her that she could jump off when the van slowed at a corner. But when it did slow, it was out in the middle of the traffic. The other cars racing along made Doro giddy. The trucks were like juggernauts and the motor scooters like angry hornets.

She couldn't hold on any longer. There was a shooting pain in her right hand. Her grip suddenly loosened. She swayed on the step for a few seconds. Then she fell from the van. As her head hit the hard pavement, the right wheels of a sports car behind passed over her legs.

# » 4 Bad Luck

When Doro opened her eyes, she thought that a rare snow had fallen on Marseilles. There was so much white, and she herself seemed to be lying in a snowbank. Her legs were frozen stiff, although the snow felt warm.

Somebody all in white was standing over her.

"Where am I?" asked Doro feebly. "Where's Mamma?"

"She will soon be here," answered the white figure. "Meanwhile we'll take good care of you here in the hospital."

Slowly things cleared in Doro's mind. She wasn't in the snow. She was in a room something like the one in the clinic where she and Luigi had gone at different times. And the white figure was a nurse like the one who had given them the inoculations.

A doctor appeared beside the nurse.

"Feel better now, little one?" he asked.

Doro smiled faintly. She was beginning to remember more. She was remembering the ride on the back of the florist's van. "It wasn't Luigi's fault," she said.

"Who is Luigi?" asked the doctor.

Doro's eyes opened wider. It seemed strange that everybody didn't know who Luigi was. He was so well known around the old port.

"He's my brother," she answered. "He's bigger than me. When will Mamma come?"

"She will be here soon. Luckily one of the Arabs working nearby recognized you. The police are looking for her."

"That will frighten her," said Doro. "She'll think that Luigi is in trouble again. And it wasn't really his fault."

The doctor left, and time seemed to stand still in the little white room.

At last Mamma came. She came in tears and haste, bringing

with her the aroma of the fish market. She leaned over the bed and gathered Doro into her arms.

Doro began to cry too. "I was so frightened, Mamma. I wanted to get off but I couldn't."

"There, there," Mamma tried to comfort her. "It is past. It is like a bad dream. Everything is all right now. The doctor said you can come home soon."

"There were autos all around me, Mamma," Doro went on. "They honked at me and chased me and tried to run over me."

"Don't think about it anymore. They can't hurt you now."

"Where is Luigi?"

Mamma's face clouded. "I don't know. They came to the market for me—the police. Madame Gamba has gone to look for him."

"I wanted to ride on the back of the auto, Mamma. That's why Luigi found one for me to get on."

"Wouldn't you like to sit up?" asked the nurse cheerfully. She was a ruddy-faced woman who spoke with the thick Provençal accent. Every move she made sent a crackling through her stiffly starched uniform.

Doro raised herself on her elbows. A puzzled, frightened look came into her eyes.

"My legs feel dead," she complained.

"They are bandaged because of the bruises," explained the nurse.

Doro reached back and began tugging desperately at the head of her bed. "I can't move them," she cried. "I'm crippled like Mouky. I'll never be able to walk."

She began weeping and moaning.

Mamma tried to quiet her. "You only imagine that, my little one. Of course you can walk. Didn't you hear the nurse say that no bones are broken?"

But Doro could not move her legs.

"I'm crippled like Mouky," she kept crying over and over again.

Madame Gamba soon arrived with Luigi. His hair was tousled, and he looked pale and frightened. Madame Gamba seemed even more upset. She was a large woman like Mamma, but although she dressed plainly also, long Moorish earrings with stars and crescents dangled over her plump shoulders.

"I waited for you at the head of the Canebière," Luigi told Doro. "Then I was afraid that the van had carried you to Lyons or Nice."

Madame Gamba wrung her hands as if she too had gone through a terrible experience. Her earrings jingled. "I met Luigi coming home," she said to Mamma, "so I told him that the police had come for his mother because his sister had been in an accident. How is the poor little angel? She looks so pale. I only hope they will not have to operate."

"I'm crippled," sobbed Doro. "I'll never walk again."

Luigi felt as if a knife had been driven into his heart—the sharp stiletto that Marco the Sicilian carried in his belt. He turned abruptly and ran from the room. He blindly raced down one corridor after another, trying to find his way, until an angry nurse grabbed him by the shoulder.

"You must not run in the halls, boy," she scolded. "The wash-rooms are down the other way."

"I only want to get outside," cried Luigi desperately.

"Then take the stairs at the end and turn to the left," she directed him. "And do not run. It disturbs the patients."

Luigi followed her directions, and he did not run until he reached the street. Then he ran all the way home. It was a long way, but he did not notice distance or time. He felt as if he were running away from a terrible crime that he had committed. He was responsible for crippling his sister. He would always be unhappy—even if he lived to be as old as Yussuf. But he wouldn't live to be old. He would surely die soon from such grief and remorse.

Mamma came home without Doro. She found Luigi slumped in a chair in the dark, cold room. She quickly turned on the light. Luigi cowered deeper into the chair. "I don't want Papà to see me," he cried through his fingers.

Mamma took him into her strong arms and pulled him up.

"Do not blame yourself, Luigi *mio*," she told him. "It might just as easily have happened to you as Doro. Promise me that you will never ride in the back of an auto again."

Luigi buried his face in the bulky folds of her black dress, and the strong smell of fish was sweet to his nostrils.

"Never again, Mamma," he promised. "I'll never do anything bad again." Then, shocked by the great self-discipline this would demand, he amended. "That is, I'll *try* not to do anything bad again."

He was surprised at how quickly his misery disappeared. He might live a long time after all and find life bearable.

"Is Doro hurt much?" he asked. "Why can't she walk?"

"The doctors say there is nothing wrong, but for some reason she can't use her legs," replied his mother, a puzzled frown on her face. "They are keeping her at the hospital to make tests." Mamma's face hardened. "It is the influence of that gypsy boy. She has felt too much pity for him."

But in his own mind Luigi put the blame on Mouky's father. He was sure that his curse had brought this bad luck to Doro.

The doctors made many tests on Doro. They pinched and thumped and tapped, but still her legs remained paralyzed. Then the smart young doctor with glasses and a thin black moustache tried to explain Doro's affliction with big words.

"I don't understand you," said Mamma. "Although I am Corsican, I know many French words, but not the ones you speak."

The doctor smiled in a superior way. He took off his glasses, blew on them, then polished them on his starched white jacket.

"It is a form of hysteria, Madame Valli," he said. Then he frowned as if little words were as hard for him as big ones for Mamma. He tapped his forehead.

"Doro's trouble is here," he explained.

"You mean my Doro is crazy?" asked Mamma indignantly. "My Doro who is one of the smartest ones in her class?"

"Oh, not that," said the doctor quickly. "It is merely that the idea she cannot walk is somehow fixed in her mind."

Mamma's black eyes began to flash. "You must make my Doro walk," she commanded.

"But Madame—Madame—" sputtered the young doctor who was used to giving orders instead of receiving them.

Mamma advanced upon him, shaking her fist. "You have all the strong medicines and magic machines and the big words," she exploded. "Why can't you make her walk with them? What is this hospital for?"

The doctor stepped back and discreetly drew a chair between himself and the angry woman. "I will get Dr. Gabot," he said hastily. "Perhaps he will be able to explain it better."

Dr. Gabot was an older man with a tired face and kind eyes. He gently eased Mamma into the chair. He patted her heaving shoulder.

"As you told us yourself," he said, "it is highly possible that your little girl has been influenced by her sympathy for some crippled beggar."

Mamma rubbed her eyes. "But when will she be able to walk again?" she asked. "The other doctor thinks my Doro is wrong in her head."

Dr. Gabot put his hand to his breast. "I don't think the trouble is in her head," he assured her. "I think it is in her heart."

"But when *will* she walk?" persisted Mamma.

Dr. Gabot looked her straight in the eye. "Maybe tomorrow, Madame. Maybe next week." He dropped his voice until it was almost a whisper. "Maybe never."

Mamma began to weep.

"I have seen many such cases as this in the war," the doctor continued. "Perhaps some shock will cure your daughter. Medicines are not enough. Hope is more important. There is always hope."

Mamma pulled her old shawl about her shoulders. Her smile was like a rainbow after her tears. "Of course there is always hope, doctor," she said. " 'The nets that are empty today may be full tomorrow.' That is what the fishermen say."

So they brought Doro home in an ambulance. Such a crowd of North Africans gathered around it when it stopped at the foot of the Street of the Strangers that one would have thought it was one of the police roundups that sometimes took place there.

A young medical assistant carried Doro upstairs to the Valli apartment and made her comfortable in a chair by the window. Then the ambulance drove away and the crowd dispersed.

"We really don't understand what is wrong with Doro," Luigi told the old chicken-seller. "We don't even know if she'll ever be able to walk again. We've said dozens of prayers and Mamma keeps a candle lighted at St. Laurent."

Yussuf thoughtfully pulled at his beard. "As our holy book the Koran says, 'Give Allah time. He is with the patient.' "

"But it's so queer," mused Luigi. "She can't walk because she thinks her legs won't move. Have you ever heard of anything like that?"

Yussuf nodded sagely. "Perhaps I can explain it to you."

From the folds of his robe he brought forth the piece of chalk he sometimes used for marking prices on the sidewalk. He drew a wide circle. Then he went to one of the crates and pulled out a squawking, flapping hen. As she struggled to free herself, he forced her on her side within the circle. He placed her head so that one eye was fastened on the white line. Slowly she grew still.

Yussuf let go of her. He passed his hand over her body in sweeping movements. He turned his back and walked away. The hen did not move.

"You see," Yussuf told Luigi, "she could easily escape me now. But her eye is hypnotized by the white line. She thinks that she cannot move."

Luigi stared in fascination at the hypnotized fowl.

Then Yussuf seized the hen by her legs and whirled her around. She began squawking and flapping again.

"Your sister has her eye on a white line," said Yussuf. "*Inshallah*—it is Allah's will. But if it is His will, she shall escape from the circle."

Luigi nodded. But how could one draw Doro's attention from the white line fixed in her mind?

He went to Mouky.

"Did your father's curse cause Doro's trouble?" he asked.

The gypsy boy was shifty-eyed. "Maybe," he answered.

"The doctor said she needs a shock," continued Luigi. "Would a shock stop the curse?"

"Maybe it would take a miracle," said Mouky. He made a pitiful face and began talking in a whining voice. "I was hurt so bad when the van pinned me down that only a miracle can cure me now. Every spring my parents take me on the pilgrimage to the St. Maries de la Mer. They hope St. Sara will work a miracle. Perhaps your sister should go there."

Luigi knew that in May hundreds of gypsies from all over Europe gathered at the old fortress church at the mouth of the Rhone to honor their patron saint. It was not far from Marseilles.

"Mamma says there really isn't any such St. Sara," stated Luigi.

Popular legend had it that after the crucifixion the two saints, Marie Jacobé and Marie Salomé, were set afloat in a boat without rudder or sails, and that their craft had drifted to the shores of Provence. And gypsy legend had it that with them was their dark-skinned handmaiden, Sara.

"Then why does the priest let us have her shrine in the crypt?" reasoned Mouky.

"I don't know," Luigi had to admit. Maybe Mamma was wrong about St. Sara. "If you go there every year, why aren't you cured yet?"

"I have to wait for the miracle," said Mouky. "My father said you can't rush miracles. They have to happen at the right time. But St. Sara cured my cousin of her bad cough. So my aunt pinned Dosha's picture to St. Sara's robe. If you go to the crypt, you will see it there. And many other pictures of those who got what they asked her for."

Luigi was almost convinced. Perhaps Doro could be cured if she went on the gypsy pilgrimage to the St. Maries.

But Mamma quickly dashed his hopes.

"Heathen superstition!" she pronounced. "There is really no gypsy St. Sara. Do you see her name on the calendar?"

"Then why does the priest let her statue be in the crypt of the church?" Luigi asked, using Mouky's argument.

"The crypt is not consecrated," replied Mamma. "Perhaps he

CERIE
Fermeture
la
lundi
Pousse-Pousse

wants those pagan gypsies to come to church once a year anyway so he can get them baptized and married."

Luigi's Arab companions were sympathetic. They tried to help with suggestions too.

Most of the boys were older than he, nimble as Berber goats and sharp-eyed as jackals. Although ragged, they were bold and self-reliant.

The boys were playing in the ruins of an old building torn down to make room for one of the new, square apartment houses. They were building a fort to hold back any army advancing from the sea. Its walls would not be as solid as those of old Fort St. Jean guarding the entrance to the port, and it would not have dungeons like those of the forbidding Chateau d'If on its island offshore where the Count of Monte Cristo and the man in the Iron Mask had been imprisoned; but it would be a formidable pile of rubble that would block the attempt of any pedestrian to take a shortcut to the alley.

"You say a shock might cure her?" asked Mustafa, heaving a broken chunk of concrete into the wobbly wall of the fort. "Why don't you push her in front of another auto?"

"No!" exclaimed Luigi. "That would be too dangerous."

"I could go to your apartment and wave my knife at her," suggested Ali, the son of Ahmed, shooting a handful of plaster toward a street light. "That would make her legs run."

"No, no!" cried Luigi. "She might not be able to move at all after such a shock."

"Perhaps you could jump at her from behind and yell 'boo'," volunteered Cherif who was a gentler boy. He was sitting in a tangle of stones and weeds, watching the others work.

"I tried that," admitted Luigi, "but she only laughed at me."

# » 5

# A New Friend

Day after day Doro sat at the window, watching the life on the street. She stared at the people below. First she could see them approaching like paper dolls in the distance. Their heads grew larger and their bodies shorter. Right under the window, they were only moving caps or tarbooshes or dark heads. It was as if she were one of the sparrows perching on a clothesline.

"When spring comes and the weather gets warmer, we can open the window," said Doro. "Then I will be able to lean out and wave to Mouky."

"When spring comes," Luigi reminded her, "Mouky will leave. His people will take to the road again."

"And good riddance," added their mother.

Secretly she hoped that with the gypsy boy gone, Doro would forget about him and his affliction and be able to walk again herself.

Since the little girl was alone so much, she spent most of her time looking out of the window. There was usually something interesting to see. Only yesterday a proud Moor in a bright red cape had stridden up the sidewalk, majestically picking at his teeth. Soldiers of the Foreign Legion, exiled from Algeria to their new base not far from Marseilles, sometimes took a shortcut through the street to the old port.

If there were less colorful sights, Doro counted the chickens that Yussuf sold. She watched Arabs go into the Café Oasis below to eat bowls of *couscous* and sip their cups of mint tea. She looked down on the red tarboosh of the proprietor, Fuad Ben Oufkar, when he stepped to the edge of the sidewalk to greet someone and try to lure him inside. He was a fat man with straight oily hair, but he had a pleasant manner—especially so when he came up to collect the rent from Madame Valli.

"It hurts my conscience to have an Arab for a landlord," Mamma complained, "but where can I find anything cheaper? Of course that heathen music down below keeps me awake half of the night, and the rain is leaking in around the window, but we have two rooms and running water—no going to an outside hydrant in the mistral like some of them have to do."

"I like the music," said Doro. "It's like a lullaby that puts me to sleep."

Listening to the throbbing drums and the wailing flute, she would lie in bed and imagine that she was in a tent on the Sahara Desert. Outside the camels were hobbled for the night, and strange little foxes crept across the sand. She tried to imagine Laila Najjar with her mystical tattoo marks, dancing in the costume that sometimes hung from her clothesline. She imagined that the Arab girl was the favorite wife of a desert sheik and that she had fled to France to escape from his harem.

It was on a Sunday afternoon that Doro saw Madame Gamba and Guido coming up the street. Her heart jumped when she saw old Signor Gamba following behind with his hand organ strapped to his back and Fifino on his leash. To her delight they turned into the doorway below.

They were coming to see her! If only she could run to the door to watch them coming up the creaky steps. Perhaps Fifino would climb up the bannister.

It was Mamma who opened the door, followed by Luigi. At the sight of Guido, Luigi scowled. He had planned to finish the fort with the Arab boys today. The scowl quickly vanished when he saw that Signor Gamba and his monkey were right behind.

Madame Gamba rushed over to Doro and threw her arms around her while Signor Gamba stood bowing in the doorway.

"And how is our poor little martyr?" asked Madame Gamba in a quivering voice. "How bad you must feel, Luigi, to have caused this accident to happen to your sister!"

"Luigi has felt enough remorse about it," said Mamma. "What is done is in the past. We will not speak about it in the future."

"And we must be joyful in the present," said Signor Gamba. "We are all alive and that is what matters. Even I at eighty years am alive."

The broken purplish veins in his shriveled face gave him the look of a dried fig, but his eyes were fresh and bright. His curly white hair was as thick as that of a young man. "Isn't that so, Fifino?" he asked the little monkey.

Fifino chattered knowingly and clapped his tiny paws together.

Signor Gamba pulled a bag of peanuts from his deep pocket. "Everybody take some," he ordered. "When Fifino comes around to you with his cap held out for coins, please to give him a peanut. It will make him even happier than coins. No, no,

Guido, Luigi! You must not eat the peanuts. They are for Fifino. Now we shall have a concert."

He began turning the handle of his organ which had a beautiful painting of a woodland lake on its front. He played one gay Italian tune after another, while Doro imagined that she was walking on the lake shore. There were red poppies in her hair and under her bare feet. She raised her thin arms in the air and waved them in time to the music. Her shoulders swayed.

Fifino bowed and went from one person to another with his little cap held out. Peanut after peanut was dropped into it. He took one out and examined it carefully. He scratched his head as if he could not understand why it wasn't a coin. Then he cracked the shell and ate the nut. His look of surprise and pleasure was human.

"You have better manners than the monkey on the dock, who bit Mamma," said Doro. "But you are civilized, and I think he had just come from the jungle."

The old *signor* tightened the monkey's leash so he was drawn back to the organ.

"How would you like to have Fifino to keep?" he asked Doro in a tempting voice. "If you walk over to him, I will give him to you."

Doro's eyes brightened. She began twisting from side to side. Fifino was even beckoning to her.

The suspense was terrible for Luigi. *Walk, Doro. Please walk.*

*Then Fifino will be ours.* He began biting his nails.

"Come on," Signor Gamba coaxed Doro. "Only a few steps and Fifino is yours."

Mamma beckoned too. "Just get out of the chair and take three steps, my little one," she implored, but not because she wanted Fifino. "It is not far."

Doro tried again. Then she shook her head and buried her face in her hands.

Luigi was bitterly disappointed. "Try again, Doro," he implored. He started toward her. "I'll help you."

"No helping," said Signor Gamba. "Doro must walk to the monkey by herself."

"I can't," moaned Doro. "I can't."

She sorrowfully watched Fifino as he left with the Gambas.

Afterward Mamma said to her, "Why didn't you walk to Signor Gamba? He promised to give Fifino to you."

Doro answered, "He only said that because he knew I couldn't. He needs Fifino as much as he needs his organ. He didn't really want me to have him."

It was after dark when another visitor arrived. There was a faint knocking as if someone was not sure that it was the right door.

Mamma turned down the gas on the stove and went to answer. When she opened the door, Laila Najjar stood hesitantly in its frame. She was wrapped in an old gray cape and her bare feet were pushed into shapeless sandals.

For a moment Mamma considered slamming the door in her face. She stood with her hand on the knob, as uncertain as the Arab girl.

Laila's eyes of Mediterranean blue stared at her. "I come to see the little girl," she said in a low voice. "Her face is at the window all day long—so pale and sad."

Mamma struggled within herself then opened the door wide. "Please come in," she stiffly invited.

The young girl tripped lightly to Doro. She flung her cape open, revealing the loose, pink dancing dress. In some of the mended spots, she had sewn bright sequins.

"I have come to dance for you, my little gazelle with the big, sad eyes," she said.

Doro smiled at her, and her cheeks reddened with pleasure.

"It's too bad Signor Gamba is not here with his organ to play for you," said Doro. "When I hear the drums and flute downstairs at night, I know you are dancing to them."

"But I will not do those dances for you," said Laila, kicking off her sandals. "For you I shall do my dance of the little desert gazelle, because I learned it from my mother when I was your age."

She began graceful little bounds, raising and lowering her arms rhythmically. She pointed her bare toes and twirled. The clinking of the bracelets on her wrists and ankles were her only musical accompaniment.

Doro watched enthralled. She could easily picture the slim gazelle now leaping across the sands, now springing into the air, now kicking in wild freedom. As Laila danced, the light from the bare bulb over the table made the sequins on her gown wink like harem eyes peeping through a pink veil.

Luigi had come through the door, carrying the long loaf of supper bread under his arm. For a moment he thought that he had only imagined climbing the stairs but had really stepped into the café. He stood watching for a few moments. He put his lips to one end of the bread and played his fingers along it as if it were a flute.

He began capering behind the dancer, awkwardly copying her gestures and steps. Mamma sternly shook her finger at him. Luigi made a comic bow then jumped back. Laila was so engrossed in her dance that she had not even noticed the little pantomime behind her.

When the dance ended, Mamma and Doro clapped.

"How is it that a nice girl like you dances in a café?" asked Mamma abruptly. "Why don't you get a decent job selling fish on the dock?"

"It is my fate, madame," replied the girl, "but soon I shall give it up to return to Algeria."

"Why didn't you stay there in the first place? What was your family thinking about to let you come here alone? You must have a family somewhere."

Laila smiled sadly. "It was my parents who brought me away," she explained. "We lived in a village at the foot of the mountains. My father was very poor. He had only one goat. His old friend, Fuad Ben Oufkar, had migrated to France. He kept sending word to my father to join him. He needed a man to help in his café and a woman to do the cooking."

"I've never seen your parents," said Doro. "Where do they live now?"

"You must be patient, my little gazelle, and you shall hear," Laila gently rebuked her. "One day my father said, 'Now Fuad has loaned me money for our tickets to France. We shall become very rich there, and I can pay him back. Then I will buy a whole flock of goats.' "

Mamma interrupted. "The rich in France don't want goats," she said. "They buy autos."

Luigi nodded. "I'd rather have a fast racing car than a million goats."

"I know," said Laila patiently. She went on with her story. "Fuad had planned that we should live in this very apartment."

Luigi looked around the room as if he expected to see an Arab couple come from behind the kitchen drape or enter the front door.

"What happened to them?" Doro asked in a puzzled voice.

Laila Najjar was not to be hurried. "We left on an old ship that sailed from Oran. We were crowded together in the steerage. Then typhus broke out. My mother and father died of it."

"How terrible!" cried Doro. Tears glistened in her eyes like the sequins on Laila's dress.

"You must not grieve for them," Laila said. "It was Allah's will."

"Then you were left all alone," reasoned Mamma.

"Yes, but I had one friend in the strange new country. It was Fuad Ben Oufkar. He met me at the dock when we were finally out of quarantine. He became a father to me."

"A queer father who lets you dance in a café."

Luigi broke in. "It's clean and Ali says they have the best couscous in Marseilles."

"What else could I do?" asked the girl. "It was my father and my mother he really needed. Only I, the useless one, was left. It was the only way I could repay the money he loaned my father."

"Have you no relatives in your own country?" asked Mamma.

"I have an uncle and an aunt. I have almost finished paying my father's debt, so they have chosen a fine young husband for me. He is saving to buy my ticket back to Algeria. They say he will never be rich but he is a good man."

"You see," said Mamma, "with all this traveling back and forth across the sea, it is only the ship owners who get rich."

Laila took Doro's hand in her own and opened the palm. She dropped a tiny metal object into it. "It is the hand of Fatima, the Prophet Muhammed's daughter," she said. "It will keep harm from you."

Doro gazed with rapture at the trinket.

"And now I must go," said the Arab girl. "The orchestra is waiting for me. May the peace of Allah be with you."

Not to be outdone, Mamma replied, "God bless you too."

Laila Najjar wrapped the old cape about herself again and hurried to the door. Luigi opened it, and she ran out without another word.

Mamma stared at the door. Although the dancer was gone, the cloying smell of her perfume still remained. It defied the odor of the garlic and fish in the stew cooking on the stove.

"She is really a nice girl," admitted Mamma, "and she has had a hard life. I forget that others have troubles too."

Doro held up the tiny hand of Fatima between a thumb and forefinger. "Isn't it darling?" she asked. "And she gave it to me to keep. It's like a fairy's hand." She dropped it into the hollow of her palm. "See, I'm a giant and a fairy is shaking my hand."

Mamma frowned disapprovingly. "It is a heathen charm." She went over and looked at the bauble. "Oh, well," she relented, "so are Madame Gamba's earrings. She bought them in the Arab market and she says they are real gold. Maybe so, but I would not trust those Arab vendors. They should deal in honest fish. No one expects a fish to be made of gold, so no customer is fooled."

Luigi looked at the little hand too. "It's nothing precious," he scoffed. "Mustafa's father sells them in the market, ten for a franc." But he secretly wondered if the Arab charm might be more powerful than a gypsy curse. Perhaps it would help Doro to walk again.

"It isn't what it cost," said Doro. "It's that she *gave* it to me."

Laila Najjar was not the last caller. A visiting teacher came and brought books and homework for Doro. She complained about the neighborhood and the stairs and the smells.

"If you study hard and get a good education," she told Doro, "you will be able to leave this environment."

Doro thought of Laila Najjar and of how she had left her poor village only to find tragedy.

"I like it here," she said. "I have found a new friend."

# » 6 The Fair of the *Santons*

"The fair will open tomorrow," Mamma Valli told her children. "Already they are setting up the *baraques*."

"I know," put in Luigi with his black eyes dancing. "Ali and I were on the Canebière this afternoon. It was full of people, and there was a merry-go-round under the trees. Ali got to ride around twice before they caught him."

The Fair of the *Santons* is a great Christmas festival in Marseilles. All along the *allées* of the Canebière are stalls set up by artisans who make tiny clay figures for the Christ Child's stable. Long ago their ancestors had believed that Bethlehem was a village like those in Provence. So the *santons*—the little saints—are painted in the brightly colored costumes of long ago.

"They were sure that everyone in the village would have visited the Babe, bringing gifts," Doro's teacher had once explained in class. "That is why we have the fishwife with her baskets of fish, the olive-oil vendor with her big jug, the baker carrying a sack of flour from his windmill—and all the others. No wonder the crèches in our homes are so beloved."

The Vallis had their crèche, of course. Through the years the kneeling king had been lost. A shepherd had broken his leg and Luigi had glued it back crookedly. And the angel Boufarèu was missing a wing. "But angels do not need two wings to fly," Mamma had consoled them because the wing had shattered beyond repair. "Boufarèu can fly with only one."

"I hope we can buy some more *santons* this year," said Doro. "Don't you think we might get the gypsy man with the dancing bear or the gypsy girl with her tambourine?"

"Gypsies!" snorted Mamma. "They have no place at the stable."

"Oh, yes, they have," broke in Luigi. "Mouky told me they went to Bethlehem to kidnap the Little Infant. But they had a change of heart and stayed to worship Him. And the dark king was really a gypsy."

"Nonsense," declared Mamma. "I never heard any such thing in Corsica. We already have the fish-seller in our set—ha, ha, that's your mamma—and old Margarido on her donkey and the blind man who found his lost son. But we must get a new king. Maybe we should buy the mayor with his striped sash too. That would make it quite official."

"But how can Doro go to the fair if she can't walk there?" asked Luigi. "It's too far for us to carry her."

His sister's eyes blurred with disappointment.

Mamma tried not to show hers. "Perhaps you will walk to the Canebière, my little one. It is so gay there now, and I will buy you candy and ice cream. You will walk for that, won't you? Pouf! Who wants to take steps to get a monkey who may even bite someone?"

Doro only lowered her eyes. "You buy the king and the mayor, Mamma. You and Luigi can come home and tell me all about the fair." She tried to be cheerful. "I'll get to set up the crèche and arrange the figures. Do you think you could find me some moss and pretty stones, Luigi?"

"I can find plenty of broken plaster and pieces of wire," replied her brother.

Mamma took a deep breath. "If you walk to the fair, *carissima*," she promised Doro, "I shall buy you the gypsy with the bear. Perhaps gypsies did go to the stable. Heaven knows that they are plentiful in Provence so I suppose it was the same in Bethlehem. But I don't believe that one of the kings—"

She halted because there was a gentle tapping at the door. It sounded as if a bird trapped in the stairwell was beating its wings against the wood.

"It must be Laila," cried Doro, her eyes brightening again. "Hurry, Mamma!"

Her mother obediently clumped to the door. But when she opened it, the dancer was not there. In her place stood the slender Senegalese woman. She wore a secondhand Army jacket over her long, striped cotton skirt. Pulling back a fold of the coat, she revealed her baby in a dress of bright red calico.

The black woman smiled and bowed. She spoke in her African tongue, which was much softer than Arabic.

Mamma bowed in return. What could one say to this foreign woman who seemed to speak no French and surely no Italian? What did she want?

"Her name is Bokou," said Luigi who heard much of the street gossip. "They say her husband worked on a peanut boat but now he's a porter on the docks."

Doro held her arms out toward the baby. The woman showed dazzling white teeth in a wide smile. She went to Doro with a walk as graceful as Laila's and nestled the baby into Doro's eager arms.

Mamma pulled a chair up close to Doro. "Please sit down, Madame Bokou," she said in invitation.

But the woman made shy little gestures as if she shouldn't. Mamma then invited her with Italian words, but still the woman remained standing.

Out of words and patience, Mamma put her strong hands on Madame Bokou's shoulders and forced her down into the chair.

"She should understand now," said Mamma to the children.

Once seated, the woman seemed quite at ease. She began chattering in her Mandingo dialect. She pointed to the walls and the windows.

"This is like a palace," she said, although no one could understand her. "In Senegal we had mud walls and no windows."

Mamma was embarrassed. "Oh, I know there is mildew around the leaky spots," she apologized, "but Monsieur Oufkar hasn't done anything about the windows."

The visitor said, "My husband lived in the same village."

Mamma said, "I don't see why he doesn't make some repairs. The next mistral will surely blow the roof off."

Doro was more interested in the baby in her arms. The crisp curls were tighter and blacker than her own. The full, puckered lips were like two ripe grapes. The chubby black hands kept reaching for her earrings. Doro laughed and hugged the baby. She straightened the full red skirt over knees that were smooth as the skin of an eggplant.

"She wants my earrings," she said with a laugh.

"He will soon walk. Then I won't have to carry him any longer," continued the mother. "I hear that you cannot walk because of an accident. That is why I brought my baby to entertain you. I wish I could do more."

The baby managed to catch hold of Doro's earring. She promised, "Your mamma will buy you a pair when you are a big girl like me."

Madame Bokou said, "He is a good baby. He hardly ever cries. And you should see how well he eats. He loves rice cakes."

Luigi felt quite left out of this odd conversation. He thought that Doro had talked enough about the baby.

"We saw some monkeys that came from Senegal," he told the woman, hoping she might understand a little French if it was about monkeys that came from her homeland.

She nodded as if she understood perfectly. "He eats them for breakfast every morning—with vanilla syrup."

Luigi scowled. "We're just talking to ourselves. Nobody on the street can understand her either. I'll ask her husband why she came here when I see him."

"She came to visit me," said Doro. "I waved to her from the window yesterday.

"How do you know when she only speaks gibberish?" asked Mamma.

"I can see it in her eyes."

"Perhaps she is lonely," decided Mamma. "She is so far away from her home—like Laila Najjar."

When the woman took her baby to leave, Mamma said, "You must come again sometime. But first, why don't you have your husband teach you what French he knows?"

As the Vallis sat at supper that night they were still talking about the Senegalese woman when there was another rap on the door.

"She is back again," sighed Mamma, rising from her chair and still chewing a mouthful of bread. "Perhaps she wants money, although she did not act like a beggar."

But it was not the Senegalese woman. It was her husband. His teeth were like the ivory keys on the church organ when he smiled at Mamma.

"I bring the baby's carriage," he explained in halting French. "My wife, she says your little girl can ride in it to take the air."

He proudly pointed down the stairwell. There on the first floor was a new baby buggy with shiny hood and high metal wheels.

Mamma was astonished by this generosity. She looked searchingly at the muscular black man in his faded blue pants and sweat-stained jacket.

"But your wife must need it for the baby," she protested.

"No," the porter replied. "She says it keeps the baby too far from her. So she carries him in her arms. She wants your daughter to have the carriage so you can ride her outside."

Mamma's iron heart felt a warmth within it. "Your wife is a kind woman, Monsieur Bokou. Tell her that we thank her a thousand times and, please, will you teach her to speak some French?"

The African's face sobered. "It is a difficult language for her," he said. "I learned it in the few years I went to school because it is the official language of my country. If I had more education, I could be a clerk or perhaps a policeman. I am the son of a Christian chief. My mother is his only wife."

Then he slowly descended the stairs with a step that was worthy of a proud chief's son.

"He called the baby 'him'," observed Luigi.

"It must be his poor French," guessed Mamma.

"That's what I think," Doro agreed. "The baby is too pretty to be a boy. And she wore a dress."

"Now, my Doro," said Mamma jubilantly, "you will be able to go to the fair after all. I will push you there in the Bokous' handsome carriage. He must have spent a month's wages on it. Such a fine couple! I wonder where they live."

"They have one room behind the tobacco shop," Luigi informed her, "and they don't have running water or gas."

"You see," said his practical mother, "they shouldn't have squandered their money on a carriage they don't even use. But they are good and generous. These black people love their children too."

To her regret, Mamma had to remove the handsome hood from the baby carriage so that Doro would fit in it comfortably. She tucked a pillow under the child's knees as her useless legs had to hang over the front. Lastly, she wrapped a blanket around her because it was a cold day although sunny. Doro was as thrilled as if she were setting forth in her own small automobile.

Down the Street of the Strangers they paraded to the Fair of the Santons. Hands waved from doorways and windows because there were fewer strangers left in the street.

"Thank you for the fine chicken you sent to us by Luigi," said Mamma as she passed Yussuf among his fowls. "Since it was so old, I stewed it."

Yussuf saluted her in Arabic fashion, touching first his forehead then his lips. "It was my privilege," he replied. "Allah blesses a giver."

Luigi went ahead and helped pull the carriage across the cobbles at intersections. Near one of them, they came upon Mouky.

"We're going to the fair," Luigi told him. "Why aren't you there where you could get more money?"

"My father is too busy to move me," replied the boy. "But my mother is there telling fortunes. I hope she doesn't get caught by the *flics* because she has no license."

Doro leaned toward him. "See, I have a *pousse-pousse* too," she announced.

But when the gypsy boy said, "You should have a little cup and then people would give you money," Mamma stuck up her nose and wheeled the carriage away at a fast pace.

The sidewalks became more crowded as they neared the Canebière. Luigi kept walking ahead to protect Doro's legs. The crowd that jostled them had a holiday air.

"If we were on our way to Bethlehem, what would you bring the Babe?" Doro asked her brother.

Luigi wrinkled his forehead as he thought for a few seconds. "I'd bring Him that piece of iron that Mouky's father must have thrown away. *He* would know what it was for."

"I'd give Him my earrings," said Doro. "Remember how the Bokou baby liked them? And what would your gift be, Mamma?"

Mamma proudly strutted a little as she pushed the carriage. "I will be bringing Him a gift on Christmas Eve," she reminded them, "when we offer the finest fish at the manger in our church."

"And I'll be able to go too," cried Doro with delight, "now that we have this carriage. I love the procession of the fish people at midnight Mass."

They turned into the Canebière.

"It is like fairyland," declared Doro, leaning forward with a radiant face. "Look at all the booths with the dear little *santons!*"

The line of small sheds stretched as far as the eye could see. Although the plane trees rising above the slanted roofs were bare of leaves, a profusion of thriving plants grew in beds along the walkways. There were rubber plants and ferns and knee-high palms—as green as if it were summer.

"Stop here, Mamma!" ordered Doro. "I want to see this pretty display."

A young girl with a woolen scarf around her neck was still setting up the figures. She paused to smile at Doro. She had built a miniature village on a hillside, with windmill and castle at the summit. Little winding paths led to the stable below. There were brightly painted villagers coming down the paths with their gifts for the Christ Child in the red-roofed stable below. The three kings were in place, although it was not yet time for them to arrive. Standing close to the Holy Family with arms raised in awe was the traditional idiot boy known as "the innocent one."

"Look, we can buy our king there," cried Luigi, hurrying to the next *baraque*. "They have a whole row of them in the right size."

The figures were set up on stairlike shelves. There were even boxes of Christmas tree balls, and bags of green confetti for sale.

The proprietor was a stocky man with beetling eyebrows that met across his nose. He coughed heavily from time to time.

He noticed the Vallis and held out a blue-robed king.

"It is created from the same clay from which your ancestor

Adam came," he informed them, ending his words with a cough.

"You should take care of your chest, monsieur," warned Mamma. "If you would tuck that folded newspaper inside your coat, it would keep you warmer."

The man shrugged. "It was cold in Bethlehem that night," he said.

"Let's buy the king," Luigi urged. "How much for him?"

Before the man could answer, Mamma began pushing Doro along. "Always you want to buy the first thing you see, Luigi. That is not the way to shop. Do I buy cabbage from the closest pushcart?"

At another booth an old woman huddling within her shawls tried to tempt them. "One franc for the innocent one," she announced in a cracked voice. "Only half that for the mayor."

This temptation was too great for Mamma. She purchased the cheap mayor. But it was not until they had gone many blocks that she would consent to buy a king.

"There are more of them," she admitted, "but it is late, so we must be getting back home. And all the *santons* are beginning to look alike to me now—I have seen so many."

Although the kneeling kings really were much alike, the children took time to examine several before both of them could decide on one with a flowing white beard and red robe.

"A king for only two francs," wheedled the vendor. "Where can you get such a bargain in real kings nowadays?"

Mamma even purchased a new angel with trumpet and full-blown cheeks. "Perhaps Boufarèu *could* fly better with two wings," she said. "It's a long, tiring flight from heaven—almost as hard as for us to get there."

Then because she wanted Doro to be satisfied, she let her buy the gypsy man with the bear. And of course she treated them to a sack of nougats.

Doro carefully nestled the figures in her lap and fondled them affectionately. "I can hardly wait to fix our crèche. Perhaps we could put some boxes on the table and make steps like those in some of the booths."

On the way back they passed Mouky's mother. A faded yellow scarf was twisted around her head, and long flowered skirts hung below her tattered cloak. She was bent over the palm of a young girl with short hair and long eyelashes, but she kept furtively glancing over her shoulder with catlike eyes. Luigi heard her murmuring the words "love" and "riches."

The late afternoon sun was already gilding the statue on the church of Notre Dame de la Garde. Mamma took Doro along the broad walk on the harbor side of the Quai du Port so that she could have a good view of the fishing boats tied up at the wharves.

Near the Hotel de Ville a gang of boys scrambling over a quay fence stopped their play to stare at the sight of a girl in a baby carriage.

"Look at the big baby!" shouted one with shaggy hair and weasel eyes.

"The baby's too big for her buggy," cried a companion wearing an oversize seaman's cap tilted over one ear. "See her legs hanging over the front. Haven't you learned to walk yet, baby?"

Luigi's eyes narrowed and glinted. He tightened his fists and started for the unkempt ringleader.

Mamma let go of the carriage handle and jerked him back by his jacket. Doro hid her face in her hands.

"They are only guttersnipes," declared Mamma. "Ignore them."

Luigi kept struggling to get loose from her. "Let me go. I'll fix them," he insisted.

Mamma propelled the carriage with one hand and pulled Luigi's arm with the other. The taunts of "baby, baby" grew fainter and fainter as Mamma walked faster.

"That's Marco the Sicilian and his gang," panted Luigi, still trying to pull free from his mother's tight grip. "Wait until I get the Arabs together. We'll sweep the cobbles with them."

"Such a way to talk," scolded Mamma, "and you have just left the little saints."

Doro was sobbing hysterically into her hands. "I'll never ride in this carriage again. Never! Never!"

# » 7 The Offering of the Fish

Mamma Valli looked over her mound of glistening mackerel and sardines to see a policeman dragging a disheveled boy through the market. A feeling of foreboding gripped her. As the pair drew closer her suspicion was confirmed. The boy with the bloody mouth and torn shirt was Luigi.

Business suddenly stopped. The man with a sharp knife raised to open an oyster dropped both into the bed of seaweed below his hands. The Frenchwoman forgot her customers and turned away from the pale squid with their flat eyes and long fleshy whiskers. A young man in dungarees raised his eyes from the *grondins*, with their huge heads, and let his slimy arms hang limply.

All eyes followed the policeman pulling his prisoner toward the mound of mackerel and sardines.

The policeman released his hold and gave Luigi a rough shove forward.

"Is this young *fripon* your son, madame?" he demanded.

Mamma bridled. "He is no rogue," she said with dignity. "He is Luigi, the son of Dorotea, the daughter of Julio. And I am Dorotea."

The policeman was not interested in Luigi's pedigree. "He has been involved in a gang fight on the Quai du Port," he accused.

Luigi tried to close the gaping rip in his shirt. "It's Marco who has a gang," he protested. "We just have a club."

Mamma now sided with the policeman. "Shame on you!" she scolded Luigi. "Fighting in the streets with riffraff!"

"We were winning," declared Luigi, proudly wiping the blood from his lips. "We had them beaten. They won't call Doro a baby anymore."

"To think that a son of mine would get mixed up in a street

brawl!" wailed Mamma. "Didn't I forbid you to fight with those young ruffians?" But thinking back, she couldn't remember if she had actually forbidden him.

"It took three of us to break up the battle," stated the policeman, "and we found knives on some of them."

Luigi vigorously came to the defense of the accused. "Ali didn't use his knife at all," he explained. "I told him at the beginning that Mamma wouldn't let him fight on my side if he pulled his knife. And Marco didn't have time to draw his because Ali twisted his arm and knocked him against the bus-stop sign."

"You see what violence was committed," put in the policeman. "He admits it himself. If you don't discipline him more strictly, madame, he will grow up to be a hardened criminal."

"I will not," Luigi denied. "I'm going to be an auto racer."

The policeman continued. "I would have taken him to headquarters but that would take so long and it is close to my lunch period. My wife doesn't like it if I am late. So I turn him over to you." He glared at Luigi. "And don't let me catch you on the Quai du Port for a long time, my young gamecock."

"That is generous of you," said Mamma. "Here, let me give you a fat mackerel to take to your good wife so she will not be angry with you."

She picked out a suitable fish and wrapped it in a sheet of old newspaper.

"Thank you, madame," replied the policeman. "I can understand the boy's side of it. That Marco gang has caused us trouble before. Perhaps your son will grow up to be a brave policeman."

He strode away, clutching the package in one hand and twirling his club with the other.

Luigi stood forlornly before his mother's stern eyes. Even the mackerel and sardines seemed to be staring at him reproachfully, and the live lobsters in the next stall seemed to quiver with indignation.

"So you bring shame to your father's memory by getting into trouble with the police again," accused Mamma sadly.

Madame Gamba rearranged an ugly *rascasse* on her table, her stubby fingers skillfully avoiding the sharp spines on its fins. "My Guido never gets into trouble," she stated smugly. "He is a good, dependable boy."

Then the man presiding over the heaps of rough sea squirts began to clap. "Bravo, my little Napoleon from Corsica!" he shouted. "Let me treat a brave hero to some of my little sea violets. Help yourself!" He picked up a handful of the sea squirts and held them out to Luigi.

Mamma frowned. "You should not reward him for an evil deed," she remonstrated.

"I am not rewarding him for an evil deed," declared the man. "The sea squirts are a reward for his part in battling public enemies. I know that Marco gang. They sometimes filch from my table."

Luigi eagerly accepted the gift. His white teeth bit through the tough sac of one. He sucked the juicy insides with relish.

The oysterman was not to be outdone. "Have an oyster or two." He picked up his knife again and cleaned the shell of one of the biggest. "They will give our little Corsican strength to overcome his enemies. I too have been molested by Marco the Sicilian."

Mamma was quite annoyed. "All of you will do well to remember how the big Napoleon ended up—especially you, Luigi." A shocked look crossed her face. "Where is your jacket?"

"It got pulled off during the fight," mumbled the boy, his words muffled by the oyster and its juice. "I'll go back and get it."

"Indeed you will not," she forbade him. "You heard what the policeman said. I'll go for it. And you'll sit here and watch my fish. Then you'll return home and stay there for the rest of the day. Perhaps Doro can mend your shirt."

As it turned out, Doro thought that Luigi was a hero too.

"Weren't you afraid of those wicked boys?" she asked, punching uneven stitches into the torn shirt. "They might have thrown you into the harbor."

Luigi turned down the corners of his lips disdainfully. "I'm not afraid of anybody," he bragged, "not even those *flics*."

But as he spoke, he knew there was something which he feared so much that he couldn't mention it. The gypsy curse! Wasn't it enough that Doro had been crippled by it? When would it end? Or would it keep bringing more bad luck to them?

"You didn't mean that about not riding in the carriage anymore, did you?" he asked.

"Yes, I did," vowed Doro. She poked a needle so roughly through the cloth that it pricked her finger. "Ouch! But I'd rather be stuck by needles than have people laughing at me."

"I told you we gave Marco's gang a good licking. They won't dare make fun of you again."

"I don't care," said Doro. "Somebody else might laugh at me and call me a baby. I must look like a baby in that buggy with Mamma pushing me."

Nor was Mamma herself able to change Doro's mind.

"You'll surely ride in it to midnight Mass on Christmas Eve, won't you, my little one? Otherwise, I will have to carry you there."

"No not even there. And I won't let you carry me like a baby either."

"It will be late at night and not many people will be out. And those that are will mostly be pious churchgoers who certainly will not laugh at the unfortunate."

"No, no! You and Luigi can pray for me. I'll sit by the crèche and listen to the bells ringing all over the city and pretend that I am there."

Making the crèche was an even greater pleasure for the girl than it had been in years before. There were so few ways she could entertain herself now.

Luigi pushed a table against the wall and set a small box upside down on it to make a hill for the windmill. Mamma brought home a roll of brown wrapping paper, and Doro cut it into lengths to cover the tabletop and the box.

"We will have to eat at the sink now," Mamma reminded them, "but it will be our sacrifice for the Holy Child."

Luigi gathered bags of pebbles from vacant lots, and Doro laid them out as borders for the road to the stable. He also gleaned cast-off wrappings of foil, which his sister cut into lengths for a stream to cascade from the top of the hill.

"You must not put the Infant in the manger until you hear the bells ring at midnight," Mamma reminded her.

"And I'll hide the kings behind the box until it's time for them to arrive," said Doro.

She amused herself by rearranging the clay figures many times a day. She laughed when Luigi stood the innocent one with his upraised arms in front of the ox.

"Look, Mamma," he cried. "He's a bullfighter now."

Mamma did not think it was funny. "It is sinful to make jokes with the little saints," she reprimanded him.

Luigi thought that Doro would surely change her mind about riding in the Bokou carriage when the time actually came for midnight Mass at the church of St. Laurent. But he and Mamma had to leave her sitting by the crèche, with her elbows propped on the brown paper and a sad look in her big eyes.

Despite what Mamma had said, the streets were crowded, and not all of the people thronging them were churchgoers. There were men and women dressed in such grand clothes as one saw in the shop windows of the Canebière. They were on their way to *reveillons*—Christmas feasts at the homes of friends or in the elegant restaurants. Even Arabs prowled the sidewalks, because they could not bear to be asleep if others were awake.

Luigi looked down at the old port and saw the lights on the ships and quayside. They decorated the surface of the water with swaying garlands.

Looking over their shoulders, he and Mamma could see Notre Dame de la Garde illuminated on its high hill.

"The Blessed Mother and Babe look as if they are floating on a cloud in heaven," said Mamma with awe. "It is like seeing a vision on Christmas Eve."

The ancient church at St. Laurent was also brilliantly lighted inside, and there was a heady smell of candles and incense—and fish.

"You go and get a kneeler near the crèche," Mamma told him. "I must join those gathering for the processional."

Mamma looked elegant for her part in the offering of the fish. She had taken from her dowry chest the red silk shawl which

Papà had given her after Luigi's birth. She had protested that a respectable married woman should wear nothing but black, so she only used it on special occasions.

Luigi genuflected and squeezed his kneeler into a space near the crèche, although an old gentleman with a cane looked outraged at being so crowded. The boy returned a glance as benign as those of the angels guarding the side altar. He couldn't give anyone an impudent look on Christmas Eve.

The church crèche was much finer than the one at home. The village, shaded by great trees, was set in a deep cavern. The *santons* were much larger and wore costumes of real cloth.

The giant bells in the old octagonal steeple began to peal. *Balarin! Balarin!* Their rumble swelled through the church like a tidal wave coming in from the nearby sea.

All the worshipers craned their necks as the processional came down the aisle. The priest put the Infant in the manger, and Luigi knew that Doro was doing the same at home.

The parade of fisherfolk was led by musicians beating out an old village march on their drums. *Rataplan! Rataplan!* Right behind came the head official of the group, but no one looked at him even though he was a very important fish dealer. All eyes were directed to the flat, beribboned basket in his arms. On a bed of seaweed was posed the most beautiful fish lately caught. It was a splendid red mullet, fully sixteen inches long. Its scales and fins flamed in the light of the candles.

"It is fit for the feast of a Roman emperor," the old man whispered to Luigi, as if he could no longer remain hostile before such a sight.

The boy twisted around for a glimpse of his mother in the long line of fishwives and fishermen. When he saw her bright shawl that rivaled the color of the mullet, he had the aching urge to wave to her. But he knew that would not be proper in church.

"That's my mother in the red shawl," he whispered loudly to the old man because he wanted others to hear too. His pride in Mamma swelled in his chest like the roll of the organ music.

"S-sh!" hissed a woman behind him.

The bearer of the basket stopped before the crèche and made a deep bow as he offered the red fish.

"Little Jesus, our Lord," he intoned in a deep bass voice, "the fishermen and fishwives of St. Laurent come to offer you the most beautiful fish of the sea. . . ."

Luigi was sure that even the most expensive restaurants on the Canebière had never served such a fish to their patrons. Most of the mullets he had seen were frying-pan size.

"Oh, You are the Master of all. You who refill our nets with fish, You who send the storms to chastise us for our mistakes, make us always live in the way we should. . . ."

Luigi remembered the tons of sardines caught by the fishing boats off La Ciotat not too long ago. He thought about the treacherous storms that sometimes swamped the boats and

drowned their crews, or spilled their catch back into the sea.

"Keep peace in the families and health in the whole household. Amen."

Luigi was pondering those last words as he sleepily stumbled home beside Mamma. "Peace in the family." I will try to be a good boy like Guido so Mamma will not have to quarrel with me, he thought. "Health in the whole household." I must do something to help cure Doro. It is my fault that she can't walk. I must find a way to make her walk again. How? Prayers have not been enough. It is easy to pray for something. Perhaps the Holy Infant expects me to do some of the work myself.

# » 8 The Gypsy Party

The more Luigi thought about it, the more he felt that there was only one way to rid his family of the bad luck. He must go directly to Mouky's father and plead with him. It was a terrifying decision. He remembered the man's blazing eyes and his mysterious gestures over the *pousse-pousse*. Facing him would demand more bravery than fighting Marco's gang or racing in the Rallye de Monte Carlo.

Luigi asked questions on the street and learned where Mouky's family were living, in the rented loft of a warehouse. No one knew the real name of Mouky's father.

"They call him Titi," said the clerk in the tobacco store, "and his wife is named Rhona. There are some other gypsy families in the neighborhood, but they keep their business to themselves, so that is all I know about them."

But each day Luigi would say to himself, "Tomorrow I will go to see that Titi. The mistral is blowing so hard today. I might get a bad cough."

Or, "I will surely go tomorrow. I should stay home and do my school lessons today."

Then, "I can't go today. There is to be a parade of the Foreign Legion on the Canebière."

Luigi loved parades so he couldn't even consider missing this one.

His toes began to tap when he caught sight of the line of soldiers in their blue uniforms and white caps, swinging along to the stirring strains of "The March of the Legion." He hopped from the curb and fell in line with them. He marched with his shoulders straight and his chin high in the air. He was a brave veteran of many battles on the scorching sands of the Sahara. All the cheers and the salutes were for him, even that of the toddling child whose mother lifted him to attention and held his chubby hand to his forehead. Then a policeman pulled Luigi out of the line, so he became a mere spectator again.

Another day Mamma said to him, "Tomorrow begins the sale of the *navettes*, so you must go to the bakery on the Rue de Saint and buy us three dozen."

Doro squeezed her hands together. "I love *navettes*," she declared. "They're the best cookies in the world, and I love the way they are shaped like little boats."

"They are a symbol of the bark that carried the holy Maries to the Camargue," explained Mamma. She continued her instructions to Luigi. "Then you will go to the abbey of St. Victor to burn a green candle. And you will leave an offering of six *navettes* for the poor. The mayor of Marseilles himself will do the same—just like the humble fishermen who want a blessing on their season's work."

Luigi did not mind his task at all. It was the best kind of excuse for not going to see Titi on that tomorrow.

He felt like an important official himself when he exchanged the money Mamma had given him for the bag of golden cookies. On the way to the ancient abbey he ate one to make sure that it was baked just right. It was, so he ate another.

He proudly bought one green candle, measuring it with others to make sure that it was no shorter. He lit it at the altar, then carefully counted out six *navettes* for the poor. He ate a seventh himself there in the church, because he knew that his family was poor too.

It seemed a good omen that on the way back he should come upon Mouky sitting in his *pousse-pousse* on the Quai de Rive Neuve, because he had never seen the gypsy boy there before.

As Luigi approached, a tall man in a smart overcoat and felt hat stopped to fling a sou into Mouky's cup, with a gesture as disdainful of the coin as of the beggar. Luigi wondered if he was the mayor.

He decided to bribe Mouky with a cookie. Perhaps he would arrange a meeting with his father.

"If I talked to him," Luigi asked, "do you think he would lift his curse? Doro has been sitting in the chair for so long."

"Why don't I see her in the buggy anymore?" queried Mouky.

"She won't ride in it. She says she looks like a baby."

"I don't blame her. I hate this *pousse-pousse*. I wish you had smashed it to pieces that day."

Luigi was surprised by Mouky's words. Hadn't he sulked for ages about the broken box?

"But what about your father?" he asked impatiently. "When can I see him?"

Mouky waited until he had finished the cookie. "I will tell you if you give me another *navette*."

Luigi picked out another cookie boat. Mouky ate half of it then asked, "Do you have any money to give him?"

"No," said Luigi in disappointment. "You know I'm poor, but I'll give him some of these *navettes*."

"That wouldn't be enough."

"But can't I just go to him and talk about it?" persisted Luigi.

"Maybe some day," Mouky said vaguely. "He is very busy at the factory."

"When will he be free?"

"I don't know now, but if you'll give me another *navette*, I'll let you know later."

Luigi grudgingly added another cookie. He realized that he was a victim of extortion but didn't know how to protect himself. He also sensed that Mouky didn't want him to go to his father. Why? And why did he now wish the *pousse-pousse* had been smashed? It surely was hard to understand gypsies. He remembered Mamma's words about the foreigners—"they don't even think like we do."

That evening Mamma looked into the lightened sack and demanded, "Where are all the *navettes?*"

"I gave some to Doro," said Luigi.

"He only gave me four," said his sister, "and I haven't eaten two of them yet. I'm playing that they're real ships and the windowsill is the harbor. See, they are still there waiting to sail for Egypt—or maybe America."

"I ate a couple," admitted Luigi.

"A couple!" exclaimed Mamma. "There are only eleven left."

"I was hungry so I didn't count them."

Mamma could not be too displeased with her son. She had watched people eating *navettes* all day, and Madame Gamba had even treated her to a few.

"I know how good they are," she acknowledged. "It is like eating sea squirts—one calls for another. What does it matter? The sale of them will go on for two months. But I will buy the next batch myself. I do not get as hungry as you."

One day soon after, Luigi was on his way to buy his own *navettes* with a coin that a stranger had given him for carrying his suitcase to the dock. When he reached the main street on his way home, he was surprised to notice Mouky frantically waving to him. Luigi hid the bag of cookies behind him as he warily approached the gypsy. There would be no more bribery.

But it was apparent that Mouky wasn't interested in the bag.

"You can see my father tomorrow," he announced. "It will be the right time to come to my home."

"Why can't I see him right now?" asked Luigi with new eagerness. "I'll go to the factory."

"No, it must be tomorrow. That is good because it's a school holiday."

"All right," Luigi had to agree. "But won't I have to wait until he gets home from the factory tomorrow night?"

"No, no! You must come tomorrow morning exactly at eleven o'clock. No sooner, no later. And I will be there too."

"Will he be in a good mood?"

"If you are there at exactly that time, he will be in a fine mood."

"Will he end the curse he put on my family?"

"I'm sure he will."

Luigi was overjoyed, but he was also puzzled. Mouky had acted as if he didn't want him to see his father. Now he was overly eager that the boy should come to meet him. And at exactly eleven o'clock in the morning.

Oh, well, gypsies were queer and had their own ways of doing things. Perhaps to them, eleven o'clock on a Thursday was a lucky hour. Perhaps it would be a lucky one for Luigi also.

He could hardly eat dinner that evening or sleep that night. When he awoke next day, a gusty rain was falling, and the stains at the windows were darkening and spreading. But bad weather couldn't quell his determination to go to the gypsies.

He put on his boots in the hall and breasted the downpour outside. The boy seldom could take a straight path anywhere, especially when he did not know what was in store for him at his destination. He took a detour through the alley to see if the fort was intact against storms. It was. He stopped on a corner below to raise his head and hold out his tongue to see if he could get a drink from the rain. He couldn't, so he went on to the street below. The gutters had become rivulets that would save the street-sweepers some work. Luigi stepped from the curb and waded through the swirling water for some distance to see if his boots were still waterproof. The left one wasn't, so he stepped back on the sidewalk.

At last Luigi walked down the alleyway that led to the warehouse. There were some rickety cars at the bottom of the outside stairway. Close by was a dented pot hung over dead black ashes. He looked into it and saw nothing but rainwater.

He climbed the stairs cautiously. Perhaps Mouky was playing a joke on him. Perhaps Titi would give him a beating for coming to their place. Mouky had always been secretive about where his people lived.

Luigi paused at the door a few moments, trying to regain the brave feeling he had had when marching with the Legion. He didn't succeed very well, but he knocked on the door anyhow.

It creaked inward, and the eagle eyes of Mouky's mother peered at him from the dimness within. Before he could open his mouth, her arm shot out and grabbed him.

"Come in, good boy," she cried. "You are welcome."

Luigi was even more bewildered by the sight inside. A tent had been pitched in the big loft room. From its opening stared more glittering gypsy eyes.

Rhona pushed him through a knot of children. Mattresses and empty kettles were strewn over the bare floor inside. An open charcoal brazier warmed the dampness.

The children who had gathered to stare at him now settled themselves in a group on one mattress. They were a ragged lot, beady-eyed and pinch-faced as a litter of fox cubs. Luigi was astonished to see that Mouky had so many brothers and sisters. He had never mentioned anyone in his family but his father and mother.

"Hey!" called Mouky from across the floor. He pushed his *pousse-pousse* with his hands as he moved to join Luigi. "It is good that you come in time."

Luigi's eyes swept over the company again. He counted ten unkempt children, including Mouky, but there was no sign of Titi.

"Where is your father?" he asked.

"He will come soon," promised Mouky.

"Sit down and enjoy yourself," said Rhona. "There will be a little party."

Luigi looked around some more. If there was going to be a party, where was the food? Even the kettle outside had contained nothing but rainwater. Yet everybody seemed to be waiting for something. An older girl with long, thick braids held her head cocked in a listening attitude. Two little boys began banging on a kettle to break the silence. Were they waiting for Mouky's father so the party could begin?

Then Luigi began to feel uneasy. There was something suspicious about the whole thing. He remembered stories he had heard of gypsies stealing children. Perhaps they were going to kidnap him. Perhaps they would put a bag over his head and carry him far, far away from Marseilles. Perhaps they would take him to some foreign country and sell him.

"Maybe I better not wait," he said to Rhona. "Perhaps I can come back another time. I just happened to remember that Mamma told me to sweep the steps. And Doro is home alone."

But Rhona smiled craftily. She squatted beside him. "It won't be much longer until our last guest comes," she said in a soft voice. "Here! Give me your hand and I will tell your fortune while we wait."

"I don't have any money to pay for it," said Luigi.

"It will be free today," said Rhona. "You are such a kind boy to come here."

Luigi was still worried, but he let her take his damp hand in hers.

"Ah!" she exclaimed sympathetically. "I see much trouble and sorrow."

Luigi thought that was certainly right. "That's why I'm here," he confessed. "When will it stop?"

Rhona squeezed his hand then opened his palm again with her strong dark fingers. "There is good luck ahead," she reassured him, "and much happiness because you are going to receive sudden riches."

"How?" asked Luigi in awe.

"You will meet a dark stranger on the street who will give you a fortune."

Luigi's eyes grew bigger and bigger. So did those of the other children. They stared at him enviously. Then there was a rap on the outside door.

Rhona quickly dropped Luigi's hand. She disappeared through the opening of the tent.

The boy looked up eagerly, expecting to see Titi come in. But when the gypsy returned, she was followed by an elderly Frenchwoman of officious bearing. She was wearing a shiny raincoat and carrying an umbrella.

Rhona called her attention to the assembled crowd. The gypsy woman's voice grew high and whining. "There they are, madame," she shrilled. "Eleven of them to feed and clothe."

Luigi supposed that there was a baby somewhere to make the eleventh.

The Frenchwoman's stern eyes swept the circle of faces. She put down the umbrella and took a notebook from her handbag.

"Have you no income whatever?" she asked briskly. "Where is your husband? Doesn't he work?"

"He deserted me only a few weeks ago," screeched Rhona. "The rogue! The rascal! May lightning strike him!"

Luigi's hopes were dashed. Then Mouky's father wouldn't be coming at all. Why had he been tricked, and who was this strange woman who seemed so out of place at the party?

"We have your request for charity on file," said the visitor, "but I must have more details." She opened the tablet and snapped a ball-point pen. "These are all your children?"

"Eleven of them, gracious lady," repeated Rhona in a softer voice. "Eleven poor hungry little ones. Here is Dosha, my oldest girl. And Panuel and Sinfai." The visiting woman's pen struggled to keep up with the recital of names. Rhona's voice again rose to a whine. "And my poor Mouky who was crippled when our van blew over." Then she pointed to Luigi. "And my oldest boy, Luigi. He looks strong, but he has a weak heart and needs medicine. You will be generous, madame? I can see by your face that you have a kind heart."

Luigi was too astonished to move for a few seconds. His legs felt as helpless as those of Mouky. Then rage went all the way from his head to heat his toes. Rhona was not his mother. He belonged to Mamma. Papà was his father—not Titi who had deserted his family. He would not deny his own parents by remaining silent. If he did, never again would he be able to look at Papà's picture.

He leaped to his feet. "I'm not her son," he cried indignantly.

"She's Mouky's mother, but I belong to Mamma. I'm going home."

Some of the younger gypsy children caught his agitation and began to bawl.

"I want to go home," wailed one.

"I want my mother," sobbed another.

Rhona blocked Luigi's path. She seized his arm. "Don't listen to him, kind lady," she begged the woman. "His mind is weak too. He is out of it much of the time."

Luigi twisted and pulled desperately. At last he broke loose. He tore through the tent opening and out the door. Rhona's angry screams pursued him all the way to the bottom of the steps. Without a backward glance he dashed through the pouring rain to the freedom of the street. His breath was coming in gasps when he reached home.

Mamma was already ahead of him in time to heat the leftover spaghetti for lunch.

"What is the matter?" she asked in amazement. "Are the police after you again? And you are soaked. Where have you been?"

Luigi realized that he couldn't tell her. There would be too much explaining to do, and it would go back too far.

He offered part of the truth. "I—just—ran fast—to get out of the rain."

"You shouldn't have gone out today. Look how wet and tired

you are! You will weaken your heart and get pneumonia in the bargain. Take off your clothes and dry yourself."

After he had obeyed her, Luigi sank into a chair. With a blanket pulled around him, he rested until his strength returned. And all the while he proudly looked Papà's picture straight in the eye.

# » 9 Invitations

Luigi brooded over his failure. He had made the gypsies angry with him. But if Mouky's father had deserted his family, it would not have helped even if he had stayed at the party and pretended to be Rhona's son.

There was a glimmer of hope left. The gypsy woman had foretold that a dark stranger on the street would give him a fortune. When that happened, perhaps he could hire a great doctor who would know how to cure Doro.

Luigi roamed the streets more than ever. Somtimes he sat on the curb in front of a deluxe hotel on the Canebière, hoping that a wealthy guest would recognize him as the boy worthy of the gift of a fortune. There were so many dark men in Marseilles that Luigi himself wouldn't be able to recognize the prospective donor.

One time he saw an Indian gentleman in turban and elegant western suit, buying a newspaper at a kiosk. He even had a black beard. And there was what looked like a priceless jewel in the ring on his finger.

Luigi went up to him and stood staring intently into his face. Here was certainly a dark man who must be a rich eastern prince. As the man didn't look at him, Luigi said in a low voice, "I'm poor honest Luigi Valli."

The bearded man's black eyes swept over him as if the boy were a cobble in the pavement. Then he briskly walked away.

Luigi stubbornly followed. He trailed him for three blocks. When the man stopped to look in a shop window, Luigi stopped too. He continued to stare at the stranger wistfully.

At last the dark man noticed him. He looked annoyed.

"Why are you following me, young boy?" he demanded with a deep foreign accent.

Luigi said nothing, but his eyes became more imploring. The

Indian wriggled his shoulders as if he had an inelegant flea inside his shirt. He dug into a pocket of his coat. "Here!" he said brusquely. "Be off and leave me alone."

The boy held out his hand eagerly for the coin. His face dropped. It was only a twenty-centime piece—not the fortune he had been promised from a dark stranger. He pocketed the coin and turned away in disappointment.

Mamma too was anxious to do something for Doro. The little girl was growing so listless. Sometimes she seemed nothing but big sad eyes.

"Doro, mia," Mamma announced with a mask of gaiety, "do you know what day is next Sunday?"

A smile flickered across Doro's face. "It is my birthday," she said, "and I'll be ten years old. Last year we went to the park and had a picnic. I could walk then."

"You will not have to walk to enjoy yourself this year," continued Mamma Valli brightly. "We shall have a party right here in our home. I will invite the Gambas tomorrow."

"Will you invite Signor Gamba's monkey too?" asked Luigi.

"Oh, please, Mamma," begged Doro. "That will make it a wonderful party."

Mamma nodded. It was good to see Doro so interested in something. "And those nice Bokous—and Laila Najjar. They all have been so kind to you. Perhaps we should ask Monsieur

Oufkar too, since we are having Laila. That will also give him a chance to see the leaks by the window. He might fix them at the party."

"There will be something to eat, won't there?" asked Luigi, remembering that lack at the gypsy party. "Will we have pastries with lots of whipped cream and ices?"

Mamma frowned. "That would be too expensive for so many," she said. "We shall have a splendid bouillabaisse. It is easy to stretch soup, and the fish in it will scarcely cost me anything. I will leave out the shellfish."

"Can't we even have *navettes?*" asked Luigi.

Mamma tapped her chin. "I don't know. People eat so many of them once they get started. But the bakery might have some day-old ones I could buy cheaply."

Doro grew more lively. The pink returned to her cheeks and her eyes brightened. She and Mamma were full of plans for the birthday party.

"I shall invite the Gambas myself," Mamma told Luigi, "and you can go around and invite the others. You will say, 'You are cordially invited to a feast at our home on Doro's birthday. And no presents are expected.' "

Luigi set off on his important errand. Right outside the downstairs doorway, his eyes fell on the old chicken-seller sitting on the sidewalk.

"Who are you?" cackled Yussuf. "What is your name?"

Luigi, son of Dorotea, daughter of Julio, was bursting with the excitement of his task.

"You are cordially invited to come to our home for Doro's birthday feast next Sunday," he said. "And you don't have to bring a present."

"I am honored," said Yussuf. "I shall be there."

Luigi suddenly remembered that Mamma hadn't mentioned Yussuf as a guest. But one more wouldn't matter. And Yussuf had been kind to Doro too, because he had given her a chicken.

"You can bring a present if you want to," Luigi added, hoping that the old man would bring another chicken to stretch the food.

He went into the Café Oasis as confidently and importantly as a regular patron. The chairs were all set on top of the green tables. The proprietor, in full blue pantaloons, was busy sweeping the floor. Already the smell of freshly made *couscous* was seeping into the room.

"You are cordially invited to come to Doro's birthday feast next Sunday," said Luigi, "and Laila is invited too. You don't have to bring a present, but maybe you can fix the leaks while you're there."

Fuad bowed deeply over his skirtlike trousers. "The pleasure is all ours," he said in acceptance for both. "We shall bring the orchestra along to provide music for the party. And the leaks do not matter now because the rains are almost over."

Luigi was delighted to hear that the orchestra was coming, but he didn't think that Mamma would feel the same way. That would make more mouths to feed—and Yussuf's too.

He went on his way down the alley to the Bokous' sagging door. The Senegalese woman opened it. When she saw Luigi standing there, she smiled and bowed three times. She beckoned him inside.

"You are cordially invited to a party," Luigi began. Then he realized that the woman was not able to understand a word that he was saying. He began using pantomime, putting his fingers to his lips and going through the motions of chewing.

Madame Bokou smiled in understanding. She turned to the kitchen corner where Luigi saw that she had been interrupted while giving her baby a bath in the sink. She splashed a little water playfully. Then she opened a box and took out two rice cakes. She offered them to Luigi with another bow.

"No, no." Luigi shook his head and put his hands behind his back. "Birthday party for Doro."

The woman acted apologetic. She walked to the cupboard and drizzled a little vanilla syrup from a bottle, on each one. She offered them to Luigi again.

The boy shrugged his shoulders helplessly. Then he ate the cakes.

"Thank you, madame," he mumbled through the last sticky

crumbs. He made his own jerky bow. "I'll come back when your husband is home."

He went skipping over the cobblestones. He hadn't succeeded in inviting the Bokous to the party, but he had made a most interesting discovery while in their room. Now he could tell Mamma and Doro that the baby really was a boy.

He felt carefree when he saw Ali and the other Arab boys coming his way.

"We're going down to the harbor and see the United States destroyers at *poste* one hundred and twelve," said Ali.

"Come along," urged Mustafa. "Maybe we can shoot off some of the guns when they aren't looking."

"All right," agreed Luigi. "I can go anywhere I want now because I've finished inviting everybody to Doro's birthday party."

"A party?" asked Ali with interest. "You're going to have a party?"

Luigi swelled with pride. "A big one," he boasted, "with bouillabaisse and pastries full of whipped cream and ices. Fuad Ben Oufkar and Yussuf and everybody is coming."

"When?" asked Ali. "What day do we come to the party?"

Luigi was worried as well as embarrassed. "It's a girl's party," he explained. He knew of the Muslim disdain for women in general.

"You said Fuad Ben Oufkar and Yussuf are going," put in Mustafa. "So it will be all right for us to come."

Luigi didn't know what to do. He couldn't bring himself to say, "But you're not invited."

"Maybe my father can come too," decided Ali. "That will make another man."

"And I'll bring my little brother," added Cherib.

Luigi didn't see any way out of it. It would have to be Mamma's problem. "The party will be next Sunday afternoon," he stated glumly. "But maybe there won't be any pastries with whipped cream and ices after all. Yes, I remember now that Mamma said she wasn't going to buy any."

When he returned home with dragging steps, Mamma asked, "Did you invite everybody?"

"Almost everybody," answered Luigi. "I have to go back to-night to the Bokous when he is home, because she can't under-stand me."

"Can the others come?"

"Yes, all of them. Yussuf and the Arab boys too."

Mamma was horrified. "They're not invited!" she cried.

"They are now," said Luigi. "I thought you would want Yussuf since he sent the chicken to Doro. And Fuad Ben Oufkar is inviting his orchestra. And the boys invited themselves."

Mamma became frantic. "All those extra ones!" she wailed. "How will I feed them? Where will they sit? There aren't enough chairs. We will have to call off the party. We can say that Doro couldn't stand the excitement."

Her daughter was ready to weep. "You said I could have a party, and that it would be as much fun as last year. And I never have any excitement now. I just sit in this room and look at the walls."

"And I don't want to tell them they can't come," objected Luigi.

"All right," Mamma decided with exasperation. "We will give the party, and there won't be enough to eat and no place to sit. But Doro shall have her party."

Luigi knew that he was to blame for all this. No wonder the gypsy woman had seen trouble in his hand. If only the dark stranger would give him the fortune before Doro's birthday!

He felt better when Mamma came home from the market in a happy mood.

"Madame Gamba will give me some of her *rascasse* for the bouillabaisse," she announced. "And two of the men will let me have all the mussels and lobsters they don't sell the day before. And the wine man will sell me five bottles of his ordinary wine at cost. Thank heavens the Arabs don't drink it. I'll make tea for them. That's cheap." She gave Luigi a sheepish glance. "Since the men are being so generous, I had to invite them to the party too. Some of them can sit on the steps. But there is still the problem of enough dishes and glasses and spoons. Will you go down and ask Fuad Ben Oufkar if I might borrow some from

5's
Thé
5
10F
$H_2O$

him? He shouldn't mind since he is coming—and bringing the orchestra as well."

Luigi felt like a man of business when he went into the café to make this request of the proprietor. There were not many customers. Three Moors in blue work-smocks and an old man sat on the floor burbling whiffs of tobacco through their water pipes.

"Mamma wants to know if she may borrow some dishes and spoons and glasses from you," said Luigi. "There's a big crowd coming to Doro's party. Some of them will have to sit on the steps. They may even have to sit on the sidewalk, like Yussuf. There will be so many that Mamma is really worried."

Fuad held his hands out with open palms. "Tell your mother that there is no need for her to worry anymore," he said. She may use the café down here for the feast. As you can see, business is always slow in the afternoons."

"Oh, thank you, Monsieur Oufkar," cried Luigi. "Mamma will be so happy. And I won't have to carry all those dishes and things up the stairs and down again. Of course we're only having bouillabaisse and wine. There are so many coming that I don't think she will buy the *navettes*."

"You shall have *couscous* too," promised Fuad. "And mint tea and honey cakes. There is always plenty left over from the night before."

Luigi could hardly believe his ears. He expected that Mamma

would immediately accept such generosity. But his mother had an objection.

"Have Doro's party in an Arab café, with pictures of a dancing girl on the front!" she exclaimed. "What would Papà say if he were alive?"

"He used to have lots of Arab friends," said Luigi. "He liked them."

"Papà liked everybody," Mamma recalled. "He always spoke well of everybody too. Even of the evil ones he would say, 'We must not judge them too harshly, Dorotea. They are not strong enough for life.' Yes, I do believe that Papà would not mind having the party in the café. Although Monsieur Oufkar will not get to see the leaks that way."

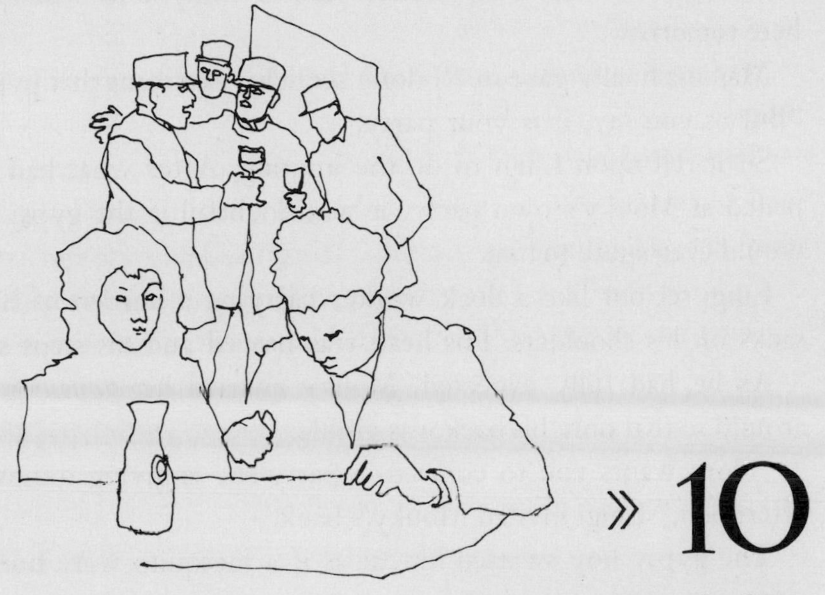

# » 10 Doro's Birthday

The day before the party, Doro was suddenly filled with distress. "Mouky!" she cried. "We forgot him. He must come to my party too."

"Not that gypsy beggar," declared Mamma.

"I want him," insisted Doro. "He is one of my friends, and it's my party."

Luigi was on Mamma's side. "I don't think he can come anyway," he said quickly. "His people are getting ready to leave. His father has gone already."

"But you can ask him," insisted Doro. "Maybe he will still be here tomorrow."

Mamma finally gave in. "I don't see why you want that gypsy." "But as you say, it is your party."

So it fell upon Luigi to do the inviting. After what had happened at Mouky's own party, it was doubtful if the gypsy boy would even speak to him.

Luigi set out like a dock worker carrying a burden of heavy sacks on his shoulders. His head was bowed and his steps slow.

As he had fully expected, Mouky swirled his *pousse-pousse* around so that only his back was visible.

"Doro wants you to come to a party she is giving tomorrow afternoon," Luigi invited Mouky's back.

The gypsy boy swatted his ear as if a mosquito were buzzing at it.

"It's not going to be like your party," continued Luigi reproachfully. "There will be *couscous* and bouillabaisse and rice cakes for everybody. We're having lots of food."

Mouky rattled the coins in his cup to drown out the words.

Luigi was angered by the gypsy's rudeness. "It's Doro who wants you, not me," he exploded. "I don't care if you come or not."

He turned on his heel and walked away with his hands in his pockets. He was glad that Mouky wouldn't come, and he had done his duty.

There was an air of great excitement on the Street of the Strangers the next day. Mamma took over the kitchen of the café and began the ritual of cooking the bouillabaisse. Beside all the fish available, there must be onions and tomatoes and olive oil and garlic and many herbs. And plenty of water to stretch these ingredients.

"The fish are just right," she commented to Laila who stood nearby making the *couscous* with wheat kernels and various left-over vegetables. "They look me straight in the eye and smell of the incoming tide."

"And Yussuf has sent one of his best chickens," commented the girl. "It will enrich the *couscous*."

Fuad carried Doro downstairs and set her on his own comfortable chair which he had pulled to the middle of the floor. The little girl felt like a queen about to receive her courtiers. Her eyes gleamed like her golden earrings.

The guests began arriving so early that the food wasn't ready, but the orchestra entertained them while they waited. Although Mustafa's uncle was a dwarf, he put plenty of breath into his flute, and the bonging of the drums added to the din.

The Arabs greeted Doro warmly.

"May Allah shower his blessings on you today," they repeated, one after another. Old Yussuf even wished Mamma well. "As our holy book, the Koran, says, 'Paradise lies at the feet of mothers.' "

Mamma later remarked to Madame Gamba, "These Arabs are really very religious. I never realized that. Of course I never knew them well before."

The Arab boys arrived dressed in their festival clothes—blue trousers and braided vests. Fuad immediately set them to work serving the guests from the big cauldrons in the kitchen. If they got their thumbs into the bowls as they carried them around, no one objected.

"Such good boys," Mamma said to Yussuf, "and so polite. I don't see how they manage to get into so much mischief at other times."

Yussuf wiped a dribble of *couscous* from his beard. " 'None but a dog bites in its own house,' " he quoted an old Arabic proverb. "Once they get out in the sreets, they will become themselves again."

Madame Bokou walked into the café with her usual dignity. It was enhanced by the flowing striped skirts of different lengths and the red turban on her head. Although her husband was in his work clothes because he had no others, they had been scrubbed to a sky blue and he wore a necktie. The boy baby was again in his red dress.

The Senegalese woman had learned a few words of French

from her husband for the occasion. "Happy anniversary," she said to Doro. Then she let her hold the baby for a while.

When the Gambas came with Fifino, the little monkey stole the show from Doro. He went around shaking hands with everybody as if it were his party. Then he climbed up on the counter and helped himself to a banana from the fruit bowl. As the fruit was made of wax, he jumped up and down in a rage. He withdrew to a corner to sulk. The center of the stage belonged to Doro again.

Three soldiers of the Foreign Legion came tramping down the narrow street.

"Look!" observed one. "There's an Arab café. Let's drop in and have a bowl of *couscous*. Remember how good it was at that little place in Algiers?"

"It must be good here," noted a companion. "Look at the crowd inside."

So the Legionnaires joined Doro's party.

More unexpected guests followed on their heels. Titi entered the arched doorway with Mouky in his arms. Behind came Rhona carrying the *pousse-pousse*.

"You are sure the food is free?" the gypsy father wanted to know before he would let his wife put the box down.

"It is a birthday feast so naturally it is free," replied Fuad. He pushed out his chest. "I am providing much of the free food and drink myself."

Luigi was now overjoyed that Mouky had come to the party—and with his father. The man must not have deserted his family after all. Surely he would lift his curse now.

At the height of the party Mamma went to one of the drummers and whispered something into his ear. He beat his loudest tattoo for attention.

*Rataplan! Rataplan!*

Mamma addressed herself to the crowd.

"And now, my good friends," she announced, "since the party is for Doro, it is fitting that we should say a prayer for her."

There was a murmur of approval from the Italians. Holding to the table for support, Mamma dropped heavily upon her knees. The Italians followed suit as did some of the Arabs who even touched their foreheads to the floor. Others lifted their arms toward heaven. The men of the Foreign Legion stood rigidly at attention.

First Mamma said an Our Father and a Hail Mary. Then she made up her own prayer.

"Merciful Father," she prayed with her hands clasped tightly and her eyes closed, "bless all of us gathered here—and especially Doro. Please make her walk again—" She remembered to add, "And the poor crippled boy, Mouky. Please heal his limbs too." She opened her eyes and raised them to the ceiling. "And you, Papà. You are up there now. Please intercede for the cure of these afflicted children." Her tone grew reproachful. "You were so strong yourself when you were here on earth. You know how hard life would have been if *you* had been crippled. Please use your influence to make these children strong again."

Mamma bowed her head. A great silence fell over the crowd.

It was broken by Mouky's excited voice. "A miracle!" he cried. "A miracle! I think I can walk!"

The onlookers froze with shock as Mouky slowly raised himself and stepped out of his *pousse-pousse*.

Luigi felt a prickle rise under his scalp and run down his spine like a little mouse.

Some of the guests, including Madame Gamba, were so overcome by fright at the miracle that they stampeded for the door. Others like Laila hid their faces in their hands as if the sight were too awesome.

But there was no fear on Doro's face. It shone with surprise and joy as she stared spellbound at Mouky.

The gypsy boy walked to her. "Come on, Doro," he coaxed. "Can't you see we're cured? You can walk now too."

He held his hand out encouragingly.

Doro's eyes were as full of faith as those of a saint on a holy card. She rocked sideways a few times. Then she cried joyfully, "I can feel my legs. They're full of needles. They're coming alive again. I can walk too, Mouky."

She took two steps then fell into her mother's arms.

Mamma burst into tears. She cried and laughed at the same time.

Everyone gathered around Doro and Mouky. A clamor filled the café as the gypsy parents forced their way through the crowd to see what had happened.

"It's the miracle, Papà," cried Mouky. "I told you I was going to walk sometime." There was a touch of defiance in his voice.

As the gypsy man grabbed his son, Luigi expected to see him burst into tears of joy also. Instead, he shook Mouky unmercifully.

"Fool! Ingrate!" he howled. "You have spoiled everything. Now everybody knows. Who will give you any more coins?"

Mouky wrestled to get away. "I'm not going to play I'm a cripple anymore," he retorted. "I hate that box." He gave the *pousse-pousse* a kick. "Let me go. I'll sell needles and thread on the street, but I won't beg anymore."

The infuriated gypsy man slapped his son across the mouth. He was kept from further violence by Fuad Ben Oufkar. The Arab threw his arm around Titi's neck from the back and began choking him.

"Shame on you!" he shouted. "You are not fit to be a father. You have no respect for your own son."

Titi let go of Mouky and wrenched himself around. He seized the Arab's throat in his hands and began squeezing. Fuad's tarboosh fell off and his eyes began to pop. But he circled the gypsy's forehead with his own hairy hands and pushed his head back until it seemed that the spine would surely crack.

"Stop it!" ordered Mamma. "I order you to stop."

Neither man paid any attention to her, and the Arabs and Legionnaires were enjoying the match too much to want it ended soon. It was better than the summer bullfights in the arena. But Fifino was so frightened that he climbed a back curtain and hid in a straw basket among packets of mint tea.

Mamma boldly strode to the battling pair. She gripped Fuad's shoulder with one powerful hand and Titi's with the other. Like a carnival strongman straightening a horseshoe, she slowly forced them apart.

"There will be no fighting at my daughter's party," she declared.

Titi scowled and muttered threats as he pulled down his jacket. Fuad grinned apologetically as he picked up his tarboosh and set it back on his head.

"You are right, madame," agreed Fuad. "A shameful happening! You will please control yourself, gypsy. This is a respectable café and we don't want the police coming here."

But two nearby policemen were already on their way. Madame Gamba had been so hysterical when telling them about the miracle that they thought a riot was taking place in the café. They came charging in with their clubs upraised. All they saw was an amiable company gathered around tables and making much of two children. Even Fifino had come down again and was helping himself to the remnants left in a bowl that someone had dropped in the excitement.

"You have made a mistake, gentlemen," said Fuad genially. "There is no trouble here—only a quiet birthday party."

"It's my party and I can walk," cried Doro with dancing eyes. "Now I can walk five steps before my legs give out."

Fuad affably put his hand on one policeman's shoulder strap. "You must join us and have a bowl of *couscous* and some cakes," he invited. "Ali, our best *couscous* for these gentlemen of the law." He even went further to show what a feeling of goodwill prevailed. "And another for my old friend Titi."

The gypsy man stood in the doorway, trying to decide whether to accept or not. The temptation of more free food won. "Yes, I am still hungry," he admitted. He beckoned to Mouky. "Come, boy, and eat with me. You will need strength for walking on your legs now."

When Luigi was able to get Mouky alone, he asked, "Your father won't put a new curse on us, will he? He seems to enjoy our food."

Mouky grinned sheepishly. "There never was any curse," he confessed. "I just made that up because I was mad at you. All my father said that day was that if he ever caught you with my *pousse-pousse* again, he would give you a beating. Anyway, you

said it was a shock your sister needed, so I gave her one by making a miracle. It worked, too."

They both looked at Doro learning to walk again by holding to Mamma on one side and Laila on the other.

The party soon broke up because few felt at ease with two policemen present.

Titi went away leading Mouky by the hand, like a proper father. Ah, one must make the best of things. Perhaps the boy would do better at peddling than begging.

The Arab boys raced away, happy to be freed from the bonds of hospitality. They mischievously knocked at doorways along the sidewalk. They were themselves again.

Late that night the children were still awake and talking over the party with Mamma.

She nodded toward Papà's picture on the wall. "You see, my little ones," she said, "Papà is still taking care of us even if he is no longer here. He helped to cure Doro."

"But it wasn't really a miracle," remonstrated Luigi. "Mouky could walk all the time. It was his parents who made him pretend he was crippled. And the doctor said that all Doro needed was a shock."

Mamma did not see it that way at all. She carefully straightened the frame of Papà's picture on the wall. "There are different kinds of miracles," she explained. "This one was a miracle of many hearts."

# » Glossary

| | |
|---|---|
| Allah: | God |
| *allées:* | roadways |
| *baraques:* | booths |
| bouillabaisse: | a fish chowder |
| burnoose: | a long cloak with hood |
| *carissima:* | dearest |
| *couscous:* | a North African stew |
| *croissants:* | crescent-shaped rolls |
| *figuiers:* | fig trees |
| *flic:* | French slang for a policeman |
| *fripon:* | a rogue |
| *grondin:* | a gurnard fish |
| kiosk: | a small structure often used as a newsstand |
| Koran: | the sacred book of the Muslims |
| madame: | Mrs., madam |
| Mandingo: | a Senegalese dialect |
| *matelot:* | a sailor |
| mistral: | a strong, cold northerly wind |
| Muhammad: | the Muslim prophet |
| monsieur: | Mr., sir |
| *navettes:* | boat-shaped cookies |
| parvis: | an open space |

| | |
|---|---|
| *Père Noël:* | Father Christmas |
| *poste:* | a station or position |
| *pousse-pousse:* | a rickshaw, a baby carriage |
| *rascasse:* | a Mediterranean fish |
| *réveillon:* | a Christmas midnight feast |
| *santons:* | handmade Nativity figures |
| *signor:* | Mr., sir |
| tarboosh: | a small brimless cap worn by Arabs |